FOXY IN LINGERIE

Lingerie #10

PENELOPE SKY

Contents

Hartwick Publishing

Foxy in Lingerie

Copyright © 2018 by Penelope Sky

ONE

Crow

The second I hung up on Bones, I called my brother. It didn't make sense for Bones to lie to me about this, not after three months of silence. If he wanted to take revenge on me for keeping him away from my daughter, there would be no reason to wait this long. And even if it was a trap, I couldn't take the risk of not acting.

Not when my only son was at risk.

Bones was right about where Conway was that evening. He also was right about my daughter-in-law. He was a hitman for a living, so it made sense he would know about the hit before it happened.

And if he really wanted to kill me and my family, he knew exactly where I lived.

He could have killed all of us by now.

Cane answered. "Yes?"

I ignored his attitude because it wasn't important right now. "I'm only going to say this once. No questions asked."

"Shit…what is it?"

"Skull Kings hired a crew to take out Conway. They're hitting him at the end of the banquet. They're also planning to hit Sapphire too, at their home in Verona. Get the chopper ready, organize the crew and the artillery in Milan. I'll meet you in seven minutes. I need to call Conway." On the outside, I seemed to be calm, issuing orders without letting my voice shake. But the truth was, I was absolutely terrified. When my daughter was taken, my hands trembled. And now that my only son was at risk, I was even more scared. I didn't know who I was up against and I had no idea what provoked this hit, but that wouldn't change anything. I had to save my son—even if it claimed my life.

"Got it." Cane hung up.

I called Conway next, the tremors starting in my hands.

Voice mail.

"You've got to be fucking kidding me." I called three more times, and each time, it went to voice mail.

He must have silenced it.

I texted him, knowing the message would be on the front of his screen when he looked at his phone, unless it was drowned by messages from other people.

Shit.

I ran to the artillery room downstairs, running past Lars on the stairway without giving any explanation of the terror that gripped my heart. I pulled on the bulletproof vest, grabbed two pistols, my rifle, and my shotgun, and then prepared to leave.

I forgot about Button.

I halted at the entryway, unsure what I would say to my wife. I didn't want to tell her the truth, that our son, daughter-in-law, and future grandbaby were all at risk. I was tempted to walk out of there without giving her any explanation, to protect her as long as I could.

"Crow?"

I heard her voice from behind me, and I slowly turned around.

One look at my face told her something was terribly wrong. "Lars told me you were running around the house like a madman—" She looked at all the weapons that covered my body, and instantly, her eyes watered with unshed tears. "What's happened?"

"I don't have time, Button. I have to go." I opened the door and walked out.

She followed me. "Crow! Let me——"

"No." I got to the car and stuffed the guns in the trunk. "There's no time. I have to leave."

"Who is it?" she whispered. "Please don't say——"

"Conway."

She covered her face, the tears falling. "No…" My wife was tough, hard as steel, but when it came to her kids, it was a different story. "God, no. What——"

"I don't have time." I slammed the trunk. "Skull Kings put a hit on him. That's all I know. Cane and I have to leave for Milan now."

She kept crying, but she didn't try to stop me from leaving. She followed me to the driver's side of the car. "Bring our son back, Crow. Please."

"I will, Button. You know I will." I didn't kiss her goodbye or hug her to comfort her. I didn't look at her again as I shut the door, started the engine, and sped out of the driveway, hitting seventy within three seconds. I didn't glance at her in the rearview mirror, unable to look at the mother of my children.

The mother of my son.

TWO

Vanessa

Antonio and I were taking it slow.

I still hadn't kissed him yet.

He'd tried a few times, after he'd said goodnight to me after dinner.

But I never said yes.

No matter how much time had passed, it always seemed too soon. It seemed like Bones just said goodbye to me at the little house we'd stayed in. It seemed like he was just in my bed the night before. Sometimes when I slept, I thought I smelled him on my sheets…even though that wasn't possible.

Would I ever be over him?

Maybe it wasn't possible.

I was sitting at the easel in my apartment, examining a painting I'd made that morning. It wasn't my best work, and I was tempted to throw it in the dumpster and forget it ever happened. I'd been selling so many pieces that I was anxious to replace them, but feeling rushed stifled my work. I couldn't be creative when there was so much pressure to produce new pieces.

But there were worse things.

My phone rang, and my mom's name was on the screen. It was unlike her to call me at this time of night, so I answered right away. "Hey, Mama."

Her long silence before she spoke was a dead giveaway that something was wrong. "Vanessa…I don't know how to say this. I'm not even entirely sure what's happening right now…" Her tone was heavy with sorrow, so full of pain that it weighed down her voice.

"What is it?" I asked, my voice shaking.

"Your father and uncle left about forty minutes ago. They didn't have time to explain. But from what I understand, someone has put a hit on Conway and Sapphire. They're making their move tonight, as we speak…"

I covered my mouth, stifling my cry. "Oh my god…"

"Your father is a powerful man. Strongest man I know. He'll get Conway…but I'm so scared. I'm a mess right now."

"We have to get to Milan, Mama. We've gotta leave now."

"It's a five-hour drive. We'll never make it in time."

"But we still need to be there. I'll pick you up, alright?"

"I don't know…"

"Mama, I'm driving to Milan whether you come with me or not. If Father saves Conway, I want to be there. If he doesn't…I'll avenge them both myself. You need to come with me too."

Mama took a deep breath over the phone. "You're right. I know where all the guns are."

"I'll get there as soon as I can."

THREE

Crow

The chopper landed in Milan at the rendezvous point with the other men, along with the tanks and equipment we needed. We were going into a hostile situation with no information at all. We could be up against four men or forty. No idea. We had to be prepared for anything.

Cane and I got into the Hummer with our men in the back.

"Is Carter meeting us at the site?"

Cane had a beanie pulled over his head, dressed in all black with the vest over his clothes. "I want to keep my son out of this, Crow."

When we rescued Vanessa, all of us were involved. Even Button was involved. But this was different, since this was a hit by the Skull Kings, the most ruthless organization in

Italy. Cane and I were well-acquainted with them. They were monsters in the dark. I loved my wife dearly, but she didn't have what it took to stand up to men like that.

He continued. "If I die, I need him to take care of Adelina and Carmen…as well as Pearl and Vanessa."

If both of us died, Carter would be the last man of the Barsetti line. "You're right."

"Thanks."

I was behind the wheel, driving through the quiet streets of Milan. It was only nine in the evening and there should be more people out, but it was a ghost town. It was alarming. "Why is it so quiet?"

Cane scanned the area then spoke into the radio.

One of our guys spoke back. "Some of the streets are blocked off by police. Must be for the banquet Conway's attending."

Cane looked at me, his eyebrow raised.

"I wonder if it's really the police or them," I said out loud.

Cane nodded. "It could go either way. Were you able to get a hold of Conway?"

I shook my head then pulled over to the side of the street next to the curb. "His phone is on silent. I left a text message so it'll be on his screen right away."

Cane's phone rang, and he answered immediately without checking to see who it was. "Cane."

The guy was audible to my ears through the phone. "We just hit the house in Verona. She's not here."

"What?" he snapped, his nostrils flaring. "Are you sure?"

"Yes. There was a struggle. Front door was left open."

"Shit," Cane said. "Blood?"

My chest suddenly tightened, the pain searing me from the inside out.

"No," he answered. "I'm not sure when this happened. We may have just missed them."

"Find some clues, and figure out where the hell they went." Cane hung up then gripped his skull. "Shit."

"Fuck. We were too late." I kept my hands on the wheel, but I felt a momentary jolt of weakness in my fingers and legs. My daughter-in-law had been taken, and I didn't save her. I didn't do my job. I didn't protect my grand-baby. Even if I saved my son, he would never get over this. My temper snapped, and I punched the steering wheel, making a horn ring out.

"Stop!" Cane pulled my hand back. "We don't have time for this."

"Maybe you should go back and see if you can figure it

out," I said. "She's a Barsetti... I can't let anything happen to her. I love her like a daughter."

"Crow." He gripped my shoulder. "There's no time for that. Whatever is done is done. Hopefully, our guys can pick up their trace."

"Shit." I gripped my skull, the rage starting to make me shake. I would slit the throat of every single man who laid a hand on her. I wouldn't stop until she was avenged.

"This is the new plan," Cane said, keeping me grounded. "We get Conway first. He might know something."

"He doesn't know anything," I hissed. "He's completely unaware."

"I mean about Sapphire. He might have a tracker on her. I've still got one on Adelina to this day."

And I had one on Button. It wasn't about crazy possessiveness, but for situations like this. I'd worked so hard to have a quiet life, and now all that had been taken from me. I wanted to raise a family and keep them safe. But no matter what, I kept getting dragged into this. I got rid of Bones, and I still wound up here. "You're right."

"I know I am. Now let's do this." He pushed the door open and hopped out, his automatic rifle held at the ready.

We met with the second group of troops, making twelve

of us altogether. That was all I could round up on such short notice. There were more men, but there weren't enough of them who wanted the money enough to risk their lives. I hadn't lied about the situation we were getting into, so some of them turned down the offer.

But when it came to Cane and me, we were as strong as five men each.

Especially when my son's life was on the line.

Silent and with impeccable stealth, we moved down the street and approached the banquet from the back entrance of the building, knowing they would strike from the rear instead of completely in the open. They would probably lure Conway out the side entrance by pulling some stunt.

Unless he finally looked at his phone.

We stopped at the corner and peered across the street. Just as I expected, there were black cars parked everywhere, providing adequate coverage on every single corner. We were surrounded on all sides. Our only option was to break into three different teams and move simultaneously.

"Fuck," Cane said. "They don't give a shit, do they?"

"No...they don't." These guys were willing to take down a celebrity even when hordes of people were gathered at the entrance on the next street. They obviously thought they were above the law, that they could disappear into the night without any questions asked.

Who were we dealing with?

"Did Bones say who these guys were?"

"No." But in his defense, I didn't give him much of a chance. "We'll break into three teams. I don't see any other way around it."

"Neither do I," Cane said. "But I've got to say…the odds aren't in our favor. We've been through some tough shit, but this…I've got a bad feeling about it." He stared out at the street, his jaw clenched tightly.

"You don't have to do this, Cane. I know you have your own family." I wouldn't judge him if he backed out. He had a wife and two kids, a family that would be devastated if something happened to him. "But I have to do this…even if I don't make it." I wouldn't turn away just because the odds were overwhelming. I'd rather die saving my son than live a life without him.

Cane turned back to me, a pained look still on his face. "No. Conway is like a son to me. I'm here to the end. I just don't have high hopes this time…not that I ever really did before."

I nodded, appreciating what he said more than I could articulate in words. I extended my hand.

He took it then pulled me in for a one-armed embrace. "If we don't make it—"

"I know." I patted the back of his head. "I love you too."

FOUR

Bones

When Max and I arrived, the gunshots were already flying.

Police stayed back, understanding this wasn't their fight, and if they wanted to go home to their families, they needed to keep looking the other way, even if the media didn't understand what was going on.

Men hid behind their cars, firing shots across the street. When Max and I came onto the scene, heavily armed with every intention of killing everyone on that block, people had already broken into three different groups. The right corner had two sets of men firing back and forth from their Hummers.

Another car was situated next to the back alley, and as we turned the corner, we saw two men drag Conway by both arms out of the alleyway. Conway was beaten up pretty badly, bleeding from his nose and mouth with two black eyes. He'd obviously put up a fight before they finally beat him into submission.

Max crouched beside me, eyeing the scene from behind the dumpster. "Looks like they got him."

"And we can't let them get away." I watched them shove Conway's body into the back of an SUV, his arms cuffed behind his back like a criminal. Once those guys were on the road and out of the city, they would be untraceable.

"Where are the Barsettis?"

"No idea." They had either already been killed, or they were caught up in another battle. There were a lot of men on both sides, both fighting to the death. Bodies were in the middle of the street, their blood draining into the gutters.

Just when the car holding Conway was about to pull out, Crow appeared. With a semiautomatic, he emerged from the other side of the street and blasted the front passenger door, putting rounds into the bulletproof glass. Out in the open and completely vulnerable, he was about to be shot any second.

"What the hell is he doing?" Max asked.

"His last-ditch effort." I prepared to run into the street. "He knows he's gonna be taken down. But he'd rather die than let them get away with Conway."

"Still—"

"Cover me."

"Are you insane?"

I was already gone.

The car came to a halt, the hot tires squealing against the asphalt. The driver popped the door open and pointed his shotgun over the hood of the car, aimed right at Crow. Before he could fire, Crow shot first.

Headshot.

The guy fell quickly.

Crow moved to the car, desperate to get Conway out.

Another door flew open, and a man shoved his boot into Crow's body, making him fall back and hit the street. The gun left his hands.

Crow scrambled for the gun, but he wasn't quick enough.

The man kicked the gun away then pointed his pistol right at Crow's face, his finger about to squeeze the trigger.

Instead of being afraid, Crow stared down the barrel of the gun, embracing death with the dignity of a true man. His life probably flashed before his eyes, thinking of his wife and kids. But not once did he beg for his life. Not once did he even grimace.

The man smiled before he pulled the trigger.

But I got there first.

The bullet hit me right in the shoulder, and at point-blank, it hurt like a bitch. I felt my body shift back with the momentum of the bullet. The firepower was immense, and even though I'd been shot dozens of times, this hurt the most. It was the first time I'd taken a bullet meant for someone else.

Maybe that was why it hurt so badly.

I recovered quickly, the adrenaline stronger than the pain. I felt the blood explode out of my body, felt my muscle weaken from the tear in my flesh. I pointed my gun right up to the guy's neck and fired, killing him with three bullets that made his body go limp.

I didn't have time to help Crow to his feet or retrieve the gun he'd dropped. I pulled the pistol out of my holster and tossed it at him without even making eye contact with him.

I heard him catch it.

I yanked the back door open and found Conway inside, barely conscious. I turned around to Crow. "Get in and take off."

Crow aimed the pistol and shot the man who was coming out of the other building. Another came at us, but Max got him. He turned to me, only half paying attention to me while his mind was on the chaos around us. "You're gonna bleed out and die—"

Two men swarmed us at that moment, and together we shot them down in their tracks. Another group of men came at us, all with semiautomatics and shotguns.

I kicked the car door shut, protecting Conway with the bulletproof casing.

The rage I'd been born with came into play. I'd just taken a bullet for a man that I hated, my brother was risking his life to save this family that viewed me as trash, and the pain in my shoulder was agonizing. The bullet must have hit an artery because I slowly started to grow weaker.

And I hated feeling weak.

I took out all of them by myself, kicked the gun away from one guy on his knees, and slashed his throat with my blade. I enjoyed every second of it, enjoyed watching him scream for his life as the blood muffled his words.

I kept going, taking down every single asshole who'd brought this hell upon us.

Crow stayed with me, shooting down the men on the other side of the street. Between him and Max, they were able to cover so I could mutilate everyone who was stupid enough to challenge me.

When there were only a few survivors left, I didn't listen to their pleas for help. I didn't grant them the mercy they asked for. Now that I'd lost everything, I didn't understand what compassion was anymore.

I snapped the neck of each one, loving the crack of the bones in my ears.

I stared at the limp bodies at my feet, saw the graveyard I'd created. I took out more men than anyone else, simply because I enjoyed it the most. I had nothing else to live for. Whether I lived or died, it didn't make a difference.

The weakness overwhelmed me, and I felt my knees give out. Instead of falling like a broken soldier, I moved to my knees. My vision began to blur. The ground seemed to rise up and hit me in the face.

"Cane!" Crow's voice erupted in my ears. "Help me carry him."

"No," Cane said. "Let him die—"

"Help me," Crow hissed. "Now."

I felt myself fall forward, the blood soaking my clothes. Before my face hit the concrete, I felt someone catch me.

I felt Crow catch me.

FIVE

Crow

Cane helped me lift and put Bones into the back of the car along with Conway.

"Bones!" His friend was there in a flash, shaking him vigorously. "Don't you fucking die on me. Wake up." He smacked him across the face.

I'd just felt his pulse. "His pulse is still strong, but we've got to get him to the hospital."

"Shit." His friend heaved with sudden sorrow. "No…I'm not going to lose you. Fuck no, that ain't gonna happen."

I hadn't even had a chance to check on Conway yet. "Cane, drive."

Cane followed my orders and got behind the wheel. The engine was still on, and the car was still drivable.

Bones's friend hopped into the passenger seat.

I got in the back with Conway and Griffin. "Conway—"

"I feel like shit, but I'm fine," he said, hardly able to open his bruised eyes. "Sapphire…she's okay, right?"

I didn't have the strength to tell him the truth, that his wife had been captured and I had no idea where she was…along with his baby.

"Father?" Conway opened his eyes wider, focusing on my face when he didn't get the answer he wanted. "Tell me she's alright."

Max turned around to look at us. "We got her. The boys took her to a safe house."

I snapped my head in his direction. "You got her?"

"Yes." He turned farther to look at Bones, seeing his body shift and vibrate with the movements of the car. "Fuck. If he dies, I'm coming after you." He turned his eyes on me, full of threat. "This man is the greatest guy I know, and he was never good enough for you. Yet, he's the one who saved your ass. You better kiss the ground he walks on when he's back on his feet." He faced forward again. "Bones had two of our men take her and the butler from the house and head north. She fought the entire time, so they put a syringe in her neck to put her to sleep. The drug was safe for the baby. She's fine."

Conway breathed such a deep sigh that his voice shook.

"Thank fucking god." He closed his eyes and swallowed the lump I knew had to be in his throat.

I turned to Bones next, seeing the man who saved my life…and my son. He was still breathing, but his skin was starting to pale. I ripped off my vest, yanked a strip of fabric from my shirt, and tied it over the wound. I applied pressure and kept him stable, placing my hand against the window so his head wouldn't bump into it. He was an enormous man, at least fifty pounds heavier than me, but I made it work. I'd despised this man for so long, was so relieved when he was finally gone, but now…there were no words to describe what I felt.

I was indebted to him.

He didn't have to tell me about the hit on Conway.

He didn't have to risk his life to save my son.

He didn't have to save Sapphire.

But he did it anyway.

Now I owed him…I owed him big-time.

BONES WAS TAKEN into emergency surgery the second we got him to the hospital. I wasn't given any information about what they were going to do. The priority was keeping him alive, and from the loss of blood he'd just suffered, I didn't know what was going to happen. Normally, I wouldn't care.

But now, I needed him to live.

Conway was checked in and immediately sent for scans and blood work, but the doctors never considered him critical.

Thank fucking god.

Once everything was under control, I finally had a moment to talk to my brother.

"I can't believe we're both alive." He had a cut down his arm, which had been bandaged up. His left eye was black and blue, like someone had slammed the butt of a gun into his face. "So, what the hell happened? Why is Bones involved in this?"

I looked past his shoulder and saw Bones's friend in the waiting room. He was a thick man Bones's age, and he was on the phone with an agitated expression on his face. He rubbed his temple, clearly distraught over what had just happened. "I stepped into the open to blow out the driver of the car. If Conway got away, I knew I would never find him again. It was stupid and suicidal, but I didn't know what else to do. I just had to stop them. That's when a guy kicked the gun from my hand and pushed me to the ground." I looked away from my brother, remembering that moment clearly because time had slowed down. I pictured my wife as a widow, spending the rest of her life alone and mourning me. I pictured my daughter's children, my grandkids I would never meet. I thought of the life I wouldn't experience because my time had been cut short. "I thought that was the end, Cane. Bones got in the way…and took the bullet."

Cane crossed his arms over his chest, his eyes narrowed in shock.

"He killed the guy, handed me a gun…and slaughtered everyone."

Cane didn't act impressed even though he'd be stupid not to feel that way. Barsettis were stubborn, but we couldn't be that stubborn.

"He saved my life. He saved my son's life."

"Jesus…"

I took a deep breath, the guilt heavy in my gut. "So he's gotta live."

"I don't even know what to say. I never expected him to do that…"

"And his men got Sapphire out of the house before the assholes could take her. I hate to say it, Cane, but we'd all be dead right now if it weren't for him."

He gave a slight nod, still caught up in the gravity of the situation. "Yeah, I think you're right. When I first saw him, I wasn't sure what to think. He and Vanessa broke up months ago, and I've never liked him. Pretty incredible that he put his life on the line like that…especially when we never asked him to."

I'd put a gun to Bones's head and ordered him out of my office because of what he did to my daughter. His noble actions didn't change the past, but they certainly changed my perception of him. I'd seen him in action, and he was a monster that couldn't be taken down. There was no one better to protect my daughter.

"What are you going to do?"

"I'm not sure."

"They've been broken up for a while, and she's seeing someone else now…"

In my heart, I knew that didn't matter. I never questioned my daughter's love for that man. Now I knew I never should have questioned his love either. "Yeah…but I don't think that matters to either one of them." I stepped away and pulled out my phone. "I've gotta call Pearl and tell her Conway is alright."

"Me too. I barely said ten words to Adelina before I left." He took out his phone and moved into the hallway.

I called Button, and she answered on the first ring. The sound of the moving car was in the background, and I guessed she was driving to Milan right now. She'd probably left the second I was gone. "Conway is okay. I'm okay. Everyone is okay."

Button didn't say anything, no doubt taking a moment to breathe slowly and let the tears fall from her eyes.

Vanessa's voice broke over the line. "I'm so glad you're alright, Father. Mama is a bit overwhelmed right now, but she's okay."

My heart broke imagining my crying wife. She did the same thing when I'd been taken. Then, I attributed her emotions to her pregnancy, but I knew these emotions were all her own.

"Uncle Cane is okay?" Vanessa asked, her voice sweet as ever.

"Everyone is alright," I said. "We're at the hospital right now. Conway is beat up, but he'll be okay. Nothing to worry about." I should tell her about Bones, but I couldn't, not when she was still hours away in the middle of the countryside. I wasn't entirely sure what I was going to do about him in the first place, so I had to make up my mind before she got here.

Button finally found her voice. "Our son is okay?"

"He's fine, Button," I said gently. "Got a few bruises on his face, but everything else is intact."

"Thank god," she whispered, her voice still weak. "He's my baby…"

"I know." My son was over six feet and muscular, and I'd seen him as a man for the last decade, but Button didn't see him that way. He would always be the boy who once fit within her arms.

"You're alright?" she asked, a plea in her voice.

I didn't tell her that I'd almost been shot in the face. I would tell her later, when I revealed that Bones had been part of everything. I would tell Cane not to say anything. And I would send Max to retrieve Sapphire so Conway would see her. "Not a scratch. Everyone is fine. We killed everyone. It's over."

"What would we do without you, Father?" Vanessa said, emotion in her voice. "You always protect us…"

The guilt exploded inside my chest at the thought of taking credit I didn't deserve. "I'll see you when you get here."

"We still have about two hours," Vanessa said.

"Alright," I said. "See you then."

"I love you," Button blurted, saying the words quickly like she needed to hear herself say them more than hear me say them back, like it was an opportunity she didn't want to waste.

"I love you too, Button."

HOURS LATER, Button and Vanessa were in Conway's hospital room, sitting with him while he slept. He'd passed out from the pain medication, finally relaxing once he knew Sapphire was safe and on her way to see him.

Adelina, Carmen, and Carter were there spending time with Cane. Even though Cane was perfectly fine, Adelina cried like he'd died instead of lived. Carter seemed to take Conway's condition the worst because he was as pale as snow. He hardly said a word, staring at the ground most of the time.

I still hadn't uncovered the reason all of this had happened. My son and nephew had visited the Underground to bid on women, but they stopped that months ago. Conway promised me he wouldn't do it again, and I knew my son wouldn't break a promise to me. But they must have been doing business behind my back and something went south.

It was the only thing I could think of.

Max wasn't there, so the doctor came to me with an update on Bones.

"We stopped the bleeding, gave him a blood transfusion… He's going to be alright. He just needs to stay here for a few days to recover. We'll keep an eye on him to make sure there are no complications."

"Is he awake?"

"No. He'll be asleep for a while. But you can visit him anytime you want." He walked away and left me alone in the lobby. Thankfully, no one had witnessed the conversation I had with the doctor, so I didn't have to answer any questions.

When I walked into Bones's hospital room, the relationship would be different. He used to be inferior to me, but that had changed. He'd proven himself to me, not just that he loved my daughter, but he was the powerhouse he'd always said he was. He'd proved he could protect my daughter. He'd proved he was worthy of her.

So now I had no choice but to give him the prize he'd earned.

SIX

Bones

Like last time I was in the hospital, I woke up to the gentle beep of the monitor.

My eyes opened slightly, and I was immediately aware of the lack of pain. My shoulder had been killing me, but now I couldn't feel anything. My eyes opened farther, and the white walls came into view, along with the TV that hung from the wall. The screen was black because it was off.

The blinds were partially open, and I could see the faint light making shadows across the floor. It seemed to be sunset, the light slowly disappearing from the world. The last thing I remembered was nightfall. I remembered executing fearless men and taking the life from their veins. I snapped a man's neck, but that was the last thing I could remember.

I didn't know how much time had passed.

I turned my head a little toward the doorway, expecting to see Max sitting in one of the chairs at my bedside. But he wasn't there.

Crow Barsetti was.

I blinked my eyes a few times as I stared at him, taking in his muscular arms and chiseled jaw. His black wedding ring sat on his left hand. His elbows rested on his knees, and his hands came together as he stared straight ahead. He was deep in thought, his mind not in that hospital room with me.

"Conway alright?" My voice came out hoarse from not speaking for so long. It was husky and harsh, clawing against my throat as it emerged. Crow wouldn't be sitting at my bedside if his son were clinging to life.

Crow slowly lifted his head and looked at me, the consternation in his eyes slowly fading away. He straightened in the chair, sitting back and pulling his elbows off his knees. His hands moved to his thighs, and his wide shoulders turned rigid with discomfort. "He's fine. Some broken ribs and a broken nose, but nothing serious."

"I'm glad to hear that." The words were genuine because I didn't want to have taken a bullet for no reason.

Crow looked forward again, unable to look at me.

It was the first time Crow had backed down. I hadn't even

thought that was possible. I'd seen strong men break down in fear once I challenged them. Crow Barsetti never showed any sign of intimidation when it came to the two of us, even though I was half his age and twice his strength. I'd seen him look straight down a barrel and wait for his enemy to pull the trigger. But now the power dynamic between the two of us had shifted.

Because I'd saved his entire family.

If it weren't for me, he would be dead—along with his brother and son.

I knew it.

He knew it.

He rubbed his palms together and breathed a quiet sigh, full of frustration along with something else. When he gathered his bearings, he turned back to me. "We both know what I should say to you, but I'm having a hard time saying it."

"I've got all day."

The corner of his mouth rose slightly in a smile, appreciating my sarcasm.

I kept my head on the pillow with my arm beside me. The IV was in my hand, providing fluids to my body. The bed was small in comparison to my body. I was surprised it could even withstand my weight.

"For starters…thank you for saving my life."

I watched him, watched him look me in the eye as he said it. I hung on to every word, knowing I deserved the gratitude. Most people would shrug it off and not make a big deal about it. But that wasn't the case here. I wanted the recognition for my sacrifice. I wanted the respect I deserved. I wanted to clear my family's legacy and begin a new one. "You're welcome."

"And thank you for saving my brother…" He cleared his throat, like the upcoming words were the most difficult for him to say. He rubbed his hands together again and closed his eyes for a brief moment, struggling to get the words out. "And for saving my son's life." As much as he wanted to look down, he didn't. He held my gaze, giving me the respect he'd never granted me before.

"You're welcome."

"And for my daughter-in-law…and my future grand-baby…thank you."

"You're welcome," I said for the third time, appreciating the fact that I was honored for every single life I'd saved. If the guys hadn't gotten there first, Sapphire would have been raped and killed. Even if Conway survived, he wouldn't have been able to survive that revelation.

Crow crossed his arms over his chest and stared out the window, thinking for a long time. The silence continued, but the conversation obviously wasn't over because he was still there. "Do you know why the Skull Kings put a hit on my son?"

"No." I had no idea what he'd done to initiate their wrath. Conway seemed like a careful man, especially now that he had a wife he wanted to protect. "But I'm sure there's a reason…and your son knows what that reason is."

"I haven't asked because we haven't had a moment alone together."

That meant his family was here. They were sitting at Conway's bedside. Instantly, a dagger went straight into my heart at the thought of Vanessa being there. She was in the same hospital as me, but she wasn't at my bedside. After everything I did for her family, I would have expected her to be holding my hand with tears streaming down her face.

"I haven't told her." Crow read my thoughts. "I will…but I just needed some time."

After everything I'd done, he kept that secret from her? "You're fucking kidding me."

He raised his hand to silence me. "I wanted to talk to you first."

"Why?" If I weren't stuck in this bed, I would rise to my full height and look at him with all the power I could emit. "To see if I would agree to keep all this a secret?"

His eyes narrowed, like he was offended. "No."

"Then why?"

"We obviously needed to talk first."

I didn't want to talk to him anymore. I wanted her. I wanted the woman I'd missed for the past three months of my life. "And what else is there to say, Crow?" I didn't bother keeping the anger out of my voice. "That I'll never be good enough for her?"

He rose from the chair, his dark eyes on me with the same aggression. "No." He slowly came to my bedside, his boots tapping against the tile floor. He stood at the rail, looking down at me with his hands in his pockets. "I'll never be able to thank you enough for what you did… especially after the way I treated you."

"I didn't do it for you." Even though he loomed over me, I didn't give him the upper hand. "She can live without me. She can't live without you."

It was the first time Crow's eyes softened in front of me, that he showed me the same vulnerability he showed with his daughter. He looked at me differently, not with the look of disgust he used to wear. "You have my gratitude forever. If there's ever anything I can do for you—"

"I want your daughter." I barked it loud, aggressive, and quick like a dog. I gripped the rails on either side of my bed, needing something to keep me steady. My monitor was starting to beep quicker as my heart rate spiked. "I earned her. I want her. Give her to me." I spoke of her like an object rather than a person, but that's what she was to me—my baby.

"Your feelings haven't changed, then."

My eyes shifted back and forth as I stared into his gaze. "They'll never change, Crow."

He gave a nod so slight I wasn't sure if I saw it. "She's seeing someone."

The words meant nothing to me. "She doesn't love him. She loves me."

He didn't challenge me. "From the beginning, I could never look past my hate. Neither could my brother. Even my wife, brighter than the sun, struggled with it. I think I've always been looking for a reason to get rid of you. I promised my daughter I would try to accept you, but I didn't try hard enough. I couldn't look past our history, past what your father did to my family. But as I got to know you, I should have accepted you as your own man. When you said we're the same...you were right. I was never any better than you. It was wrong for me to judge you. When it comes to my daughter, I can't see straight. I had very specific expectations of how I wanted her life to be...and now I realize I can't control it. I shouldn't control it. I should trust her...trust her instincts."

Every word he said was months too late, but hearing

them now gave me a sense of peace. I was finally recognized for who I was. I was finally given the apology that was long overdue.

He paused as he stared at me. "Griffin, I hope you accept my apology."

I could be bitter about what happened, but that would be pointless. I took a bullet for this man, and he'd finally dropped his pride and bitterness and owned up to his mistakes. That was the most I could ask for. "I accept it."

He pulled his right hand out of his pocket and extended it to me, offering me a handshake.

When I'd first tried to shake his hand, he'd looked at my gesture as a threat. He'd seemed like he wanted to spit on my palm rather than greet me like a man. Now, I stared at his offering, unsure if I was really seeing it because it seemed so mythical.

"You're a good man, Griffin."

I finally moved my hand into his and shook his hand—shook the hand of Crow Barsetti.

"And my daughter is lucky to have you."

SEVEN

Vanessa
_____

"Vanessa?" Father stepped into Conway's hospital room.

I'd just gotten there after hitting a hotel, getting some sleep, and taking a shower. My brother was scheduled to be in the hospital for a few days. Right now, Conway was asleep, his face so black and blue he was hardly recognizable.

Sapphire was supposed to be there that morning, and I couldn't wait to see her.

I looked at my father, seeing him stand in the doorway. "What's up?"

He nodded to the lobby, telling me to join him where we could talk.

I followed him into the waiting room, which was empty.

People hadn't arrived yet, still getting ready for the day. "What's going on?"

He stood with his hands in the pockets of his jeans, an exhausted expression in his eyes. Even though everyone was okay, he seemed just as stressed out. "There's something I need to talk to you about. It's going to be a lot to take in."

"Okay...you're scaring me."

"Nothing to be scared about."

I crossed my arms over my chest, my arms bubbling with goose bumps. "Then what is it?"

He sighed before he spoke, like he was trying to find the right words before he answered my question. "When your uncle and I saved Conway, we were in the middle of pandemonium. We were outnumbered, and when they took Conway away in the car, I didn't have any other choice. I exposed myself to shoot out the driver. I didn't get very far before a man pushed me down and pointed a gun in my face."

My eyes watered immediately. "Father, please don't. I don't want to—"

"The reason I survived was because of Griffin."

I hadn't heard my father speak his name in months. I hadn't heard anyone mention him in a while. My shoulders stiffened as I soaked up his words like a sponge, taking everything in but without processing it. "What?"

"The guy shot me, but Griffin took the bullet. Then Griffin proceeded to kill everyone in our vicinity…and save all of us."

Speechless, my jaw dropped and I stopped breathing. "I…what?"

"He was the one who told me about the hit in the first place. Without him, I wouldn't have even known about it. His men got Sapphire out before she could be taken. He saved your brother and your uncle. We'd all be dead if it weren't for him." Emotion entered his eyes, a look I'd only once seen my father express. The day I moved out, he was heartbroken, and that same sorrow came into his eyes now. "He saved my son…and I'll never be able to repay him for that."

"Oh my god…is he okay?"

"I got him and Conway to the hospital, and after surgery, he was fine. He's in his room recovering."

My heart started to pound. "He's here?"

"Yes. We had a conversation. I thanked him for everything he did. I apologized to him for the way I treated him in the past. And when I told him he could ask me for anything, there was only one thing he wanted."

Me.

I knew it was me.

My eyes watered, and my fingertips dug into my arms.

"I shook his hand and told him you would be lucky to have him." My father's eyes mirrored my own. "I'm sorry I kept him from you, *tesoro*. I'm sorry I caused you all this pain. I'm sorry…I couldn't look past my hatred. I thought Griffin wasn't a good enough man for you…but I was the man who wasn't good enough for you."

"Father…" The moisture formed tears that streaked down my cheeks. "That's not true. That'll never be true."

He moved his hands to my arms and squeezed me gently. "I've never wanted to let you go. Watching you move out of my house was hard enough. Giving you to another man is even harder. But if I have to let you go…Griffin is the best man I can give you to. I know he'll protect you, love you, and treasure you for how wonderful you are. A truly strong man wants a strong woman, and he's never been intimidated by your strength. He put up with my bullshit for months. He listened to me insult him, and he never gave up on you. And then when he could have looked the other way and left me to my fate, he didn't. He's a much bigger man than I am."

I'd always wanted my father to love him, and hearing him speak so highly of Griffin was a dream come true.

"I know you're seeing Antonio…"

The second Griffin was mentioned, it was like Antonio never existed. "I only love Griffin. It's always been Griffin. It'll always be Griffin."

My father lowered his hands. "That's what he said you would say."

I wiped my tears away with my fingertips, trying to fix my makeup so I wouldn't look like a mess when I finally laid eyes on him. "I want to see him."

"Of course." Father led me down the hallway and to the right, and then he stopped next to the open door. "In there."

Instead of walking inside, I stayed by the wall, feeling my heart pound in my chest. My entire body was shaking because the emotions were breaking the foundation of my spirit. This man was all I'd ever wanted…and now I was finally getting him. He was the love of my life, and I would never have to live without him again. My sheets would always smell like him. His lips would always taste like me. Those eyes would always be on me. It was almost too good to be true.

Father watched me, waiting for me to go inside.

I wasn't ready. This was all I'd ever wanted, but I wasn't ready.

My father placed his hand on my shoulder, gave me a gentle squeeze, and then walked away.

I did my best not to cry, but I couldn't help it. My hand covered my mouth to stifle my sobs, but there was no use. My heart was crying, and my eyes were just draining the endless tears. My heart was beating so hard I actually felt dizzy. I was weak in the knees, weak everywhere.

I kept fixing my makeup, but it didn't make a difference.

Then I heard his masculine voice, deep, powerful, and full of the love he used to show me every single day. "Baby."

I stiffened at the word, crying even more because I missed hearing him call me that every day. He used to say it when he made love to me. He used to say it when he was angry with me. It was a simple nickname every couple used, but that gentle word meant so much to me, to us.

"Baby," he repeated. "Get your ass in here."

I finally moved into the doorway, unashamed of the tears streaming down my face. The second his face came into my sight, I stared at the man of my dreams. I stared at the man I could never forget. I moved closer to him, my fingers twitching to feel his skin. My lips ached to feel his crush mine.

When my eyes locked on to his, I saw the same emotion mirror my own. Just like the day we said goodbye, tears were in his eyes. He must have heard me crying outside the room, and since my pain was his pain, he felt everything I felt. "Griffin..." I pushed the rail down and climbed onto his chest despite how reckless it was. My arms circled his neck and I kissed him, kissed him like we'd never been apart.

His fingers moved through my hair just the way they used to, soft to the touch but aggressive at the same time. His other arm wrapped around my waist, and he squeezed me against him, pulling me so tight that his monitor started to beep in warning. His IV was yanked out, but that didn't stop him. He kept kissing me, never stopping. "You're mine...finally mine."

THE HOSPITAL BED was small for a man his size, and there wasn't much room for me. Most of my body was on his, but I stayed clear of the wound in his left shoulder, hiding the right side of his body instead.

I propped my elbow against the mattress and held myself up so I could look at him, look into the face of the man who haunted my dreams every night. My hand glided over his chest, feeling muscles that were even harder than they used to be. Smooth and soft skin brushed against my fingertips, the exact skin I used to claw late into the night. My palm moved over his heart so I could feel it beat, deep and strong.

It was hard to believe he was right in front of me, directly under my touch. Since my mother had told me what was going on with Conway, I hadn't thought about Bones once. I'd been panicked about my family, about my brother and sister-in-law. It was one of the rare times when Bones was squeezed from my thoughts.

I examined the hard line of his jaw, his chiseled features that made him so manly. His fair skin looked the same, and his bright blue eyes were as beautiful as I remembered. It was the only soft feature about him, that gentle blue color. It reminded me of a shallow sea that could cleanse me of my past.

My hand glided under his hospital gown, and I examined the thick bandage that covered his shoulder. A bullet had pierced his skin, a bullet meant for my father's face. It hit Bones deep, cutting up his flesh and making him lose so much blood. He could have died, probably would have if he hadn't made it to the hospital in time. My father had thanked him for what he did, but I knew I had to thank him too.

Bones kept his head against the pillow and stared at me with the same intensity, as if he could scarcely believe I was leaning over him. Hardly blinking and always focused, he stared at me just the way he used to, like no time had passed at all. Three months hadn't come and gone. Antonio had never bought my painting. The women he'd bedded had never graced his sheets. It was exactly as it'd been before.

"Thank you for saving my family…" I'd stopped crying thirty minutes ago, but tears welled in my eyes once again before they streaked down my cheeks.

He wiped one away with the pad of his thumb. "You're the only person who doesn't have to thank me, baby." His hand moved to my other cheek and wiped the other drop away, next to the corner of my mouth. His eyes shifted down to examine my lips, to see his thumb gently caress me.

"After everything they did to you, I'm still surprised."

"I didn't do it for them. I did it for you." His eyes came back up to mine. "Your family is everything to you. I'll always protect them with my life. Because they are you… you are them." His thumb brushed across my bottom lip, the pad of the digit rough against the softness of my lips.

"Griffin…"

His hand cupped my neck, and he brought my forehead to his, our skulls touching each other. He didn't kiss me, but he released a quiet hum under his breath, like this connection was all he ever needed. He just needed me, not even my kiss or my body.

His fingers felt right against my skin, like they'd never left.

I turned into his hand and kissed his thumb, feeling the heat from his skin against my mouth. I took in a deep breath, feeling the fire of desire that I'd missed for so long. I'd been in the longest dry spell of my life, and thinking about him with my hand between my legs wasn't good enough. It was nothing compared to having the real thing —the real man.

"How long do the doctors want to keep you?" I asked, my forehead still pressed against his.

"Tomorrow."

I didn't want to lie in this small bed with these wires everywhere. I wanted privacy. I wanted to touch him exactly how I wanted, to say things I couldn't say now with the open door. "Where do you want to go?"

He pulled away so he could look at me, the corner of his mouth raised in a smile. "I get to choose?"

"Of course."

"I thought we decided we would live in Tuscany."

After everything that had happened, Bones didn't have to make that sacrifice anymore. He'd proven himself to my family and didn't have to accommodate me anymore. "We can live wherever you want. How about Lake Garda? It's nice there."

He moved his hand to my waist, gripping my rib cage with his large fingers. He gathered the fabric of my sundress with his movements and gave me a gentle squeeze, like he wanted to pull up the dress and see the rest of me. "That's too far away."

"As long as you are there, no, it's not."

He tilted his head slightly, his hard face just as handsome as ever. "Now that I've finally earned your father's approval, I don't want to take you away from him. All I wanted was to be accepted by him. We can live in Florence."

After everything he did, he was still making sacrifices for me. "Really…?" Tears welled in my eyes again. "You don't have to do that—"

"I want to." His large hand cupped my cheek, feeling my soft skin. "As long as you're mine, I don't care where we live. That apartment above your gallery is small, but for just the two of us, it's fine."

That was exactly what I wanted, to have the man I loved and my family. I wanted to see my parents all the time, see my brother and cousins. I wanted to see my aunt and uncle. I wanted to raise our family there. "Thank you."

"You know I'm a selfish man, baby. I expect something in return."

"Anything." He was giving me my dream. There was nothing I wouldn't give him.

"You. All of you. When I want. How I want. No questions asked."

My mouth formed a smile. "Wasn't that how it was before?"

His eyes narrowed on my face, turning contrary and intense. "You haven't seen anything yet."

EIGHT

Conway

The doctors were reviewing my chart, deciding whether I could leave or not. I'd been there for a few days, and despite my bruises and pain, I was perfectly healthy. I was eager to get home, to put this nightmare behind me.

Sapphire sat at my bedside, her hand constantly resting on my own. She was too pregnant to get into the bed with me, her stomach extending far out and making her waddle everywhere she went. Just like my mother, she constantly looked at me with worry. When she first saw me, she broke down into tears. Just weeks ago, we'd enjoyed our romantic honeymoon, and now, I was lying in a hospital bed.

A man in a suit had pulled me aside when the banquet finished, saying that Nicole had something for me. When I followed him into a dark hallway, I was blindsided. Three men took me down, dragged me into the alleyway, and then beat me into submission. They could have just put a syringe in my neck, but beating me was obviously more enjoyable.

Everything that happened didn't matter to me because the only person I cared about was my wife. As long as she was okay, everything else seemed irrelevant. Worrying about her was much more painful than a few broken ribs.

Sapphire watched me, a permanently emotional look on her face. Her wedding ring glittered under the fluorescent lights, and despite her sadness, she still looked beautiful. She'd been stressing about me this entire time, even though the doctors said I would be okay.

"Muse, you should go home and get some rest."

"No." She squeezed my hand tighter. "We aren't leaving unless you come with us." Now she always referred to herself as two people, feeling the baby inside her kick every night while we tried to sleep. "The doctors say you might be leaving soon anyway. Let's just wait." For no reason at all, she started to cry.

"Muse…" My hand glided up her arm, doing my best to comfort her without moving and affecting my ribs.

"The pregnancy hormones…I'm just a mess right now."

"Muse, I'm alright. Nothing to worry about."

"I know…but I hate seeing you like this."

I squeezed her hand. "In a few weeks, I'll be back to normal. I'll be the strong man that you married."

"It's not that you aren't strong. I just hate knowing what happened to you."

It was nothing compared to what could have happened to her if Bones hadn't intervened. I hadn't had a chance to thank him…or tell him that I was indebted to him for the rest of my life. He saved my wife and baby. How could I ever repay him for that? "It's in the past. We have such a great future to look forward to. Let it go."

"What if they come back…?"

"My father said they killed everyone." I didn't know what the future held for me. The Skull Kings had hired someone else to do the job. Did that mean they were still after me? Or would they back off now that they'd seen what the Barsettis could do? I had no idea. But I hoped they had bigger fish to fry.

Sapphire nodded, like that eased her mind.

All I wanted was for her to feel better, so I screened the truth from her. All she needed to worry about was having our baby. I would take care of the rest.

"Your parents offered to host us at their house. That way you could recover, and they could look after us."

"We don't need that, Muse. We're—"

"I said yes."

I didn't press my argument, wanting her to feel safe instead of getting my way.

"Your dad and uncle are there, so that way we won't be alone…"

"I would hire men to watch the house."

"But men aren't loyal when it comes to money. Men are only loyal when it comes to family."

That was well said.

"I feel more comfortable staying with them," she whispered. "Until you're better."

I let her have her way. "Alright, Muse."

Carter tapped his knuckles against the door before he poked his head inside. "Hey, man. Is this a bad time?"

"No, come in," I said. "Sapphire and I have just decided to stay with my parents for a while, until I'm back on my feet."

Carter would normally make a smartass comment, but he'd been in a distant mood lately. He approached me on the opposite side of the bed as Sapphire. "Can I speak to him alone for a minute? If that's alright?"

Sapphire kept holding my hand, like she didn't want to let me go.

"Muse, get something to eat with my mom." I pulled her hand to my mouth and kissed it. "It's been a while since you've eaten."

Her eyes still shifted back and forth with hesitation, but after a long pause, she finally rose and left the room.

Carter shut the door behind her, announcing that this conversation needed to be private, which meant only one thing. He came back to the bedside and pulled up a chair so we were close to one another. "That's a loyal woman."

"I know," I said with pride, loving the way she sat at my bedside constantly and didn't want to leave me for even a moment. "I'm very lucky."

"You're lucky for a lot of reasons," he said with a sigh. He pulled his gaze away from me and looked at the wall, his thoughts a mile away. "My father didn't tell me what was happening. He kept me in the dark on purpose. I just want you to know that, because I would have been there—"

"I know, man. He told me he needed to make sure there was still a man around to take care of the family if they didn't make it."

Carter gave a slight nod. "I would have been there. You're my brother."

"I know that too. Don't sweat it."

He finally turned to me, the shame in his eyes.

I knew exactly where that shame came from.

"This is all my fault... Fuck." He clenched his jaw, his eyes black like oil. "I'm so sorry... Sorry doesn't even begin to describe how I feel."

"We don't know if that's the reason."

"Yes, we do," he said with a hiss. "My appearance at the Underground must have set them off. Maybe they started watching us. Maybe they figured out what we'd been doing."

It was the only logical explanation. "But they didn't come after you."

Carter turned back to me, his eyebrow raised in surprise. "You're right..."

"Where were you?"

"At home."

"Then it seems like they only wanted me. So maybe this had nothing to do with you."

"But how can that be possible?" he countered. "It's too big of a coincidence."

"But maybe it is just a coincidence. Maybe they found out that one of the girls I bought had been returned to her family."

"Maybe…" Carter shook his head. "But I'd like to know the truth."

"We may never get it."

"Do you think they'll come after you again?" Carter asked.

"I don't know. But I think I'm going to have to do some damage control either way. Maybe I can meet them, pay off whatever debt they think I owe. I don't want to look over my shoulder all the time, not when I've got a family."

"You're right."

"But Sapphire isn't going to let me out of her sight for a while."

"Don't blame her," he whispered.

"So I'll have to communicate with them in some other way. I guess I could call them…" I was afraid to accidentally provoke them.

"I could talk to them."

"No," I said quickly. "The problem is isolated to me. Let's keep it that way."

"We could ask Bones to help us. He's got some kind of relationship with them."

Bones was an incredible ally, a man whom all men feared

and respected. "He's done enough for us. I can't ask him for anything else."

Carter nodded in agreement. "Makes sense."

"We'll figure it out. After the entire crew was wiped out, the Skull Kings won't be in a hurry to attack me again. Even they have to be somewhat impressed."

"Hopefully."

I rested back against the bed on a thin mattress that wasn't nearly as comfortable as the one at home. After everything that happened, I wanted to lie in a real bed with my wife beside me. I wanted to rest my hand on her stomach and feel my baby inside her. It was my favorite form of entertainment, other than fucking. Staying with my parents wasn't the worst idea in the world since she was so far along. I couldn't take care of her right now, and my parents would be more than happy to get her whatever she needed. And if she went into labor sooner rather than later, I'd have help getting her to the hospital. "I didn't tell our fathers anything, just so you know."

Carter looked at me, gratitude in his eyes. "Then what did you say?"

"That I didn't know what provoked them. And now that there's a good chance you had nothing to do with it, I'm glad I didn't tell them. But you need to get rid of that girl and never get involved with that shit again. Where is she, by the way?"

"Chained up at the house. One of my maids is keeping an eye on her."

"Witnesses?" I asked coldly.

"I had no other choice," he countered. "I've been here for the past three days. It's not like I could bring her with me."

I looked away, knowing he was right. "Get rid of her and forget her."

"Amen," he said. "And let's figure out what the problem is with the Skull Kings. They're psychopaths, but they'll respond to a good deal."

"Yeah."

"And then whatever answer we get, we'll pass it on to the family."

"Alright," I said in agreement.

"I don't want to tell our fathers about my current situation because they'll get involved in it. And after everything they've been through, I don't want to put them through any more bullshit."

"I agree."

Carter leaned back in the chair, finally relaxing now that the difficult conversation was over. His hands rested on his thighs. "I can't believe Bones did all that. You would all be dead right now if he hadn't."

"I know."

"What do you think is gonna happen?"

I knew my sister loved him, still loved him after all this time. And if Bones put his life on the line for assholes who treated him like trash, then he must still love her. "I think Bones is going to be part of our lives…for a very long time."

NINE

Bones

Vanessa had fallen asleep in my arms, her earlier sobs bringing her to exhaustion. She fit against me just the way she used to, even in the small and uncomfortable bed. Her cheek was on my chest, while her arm was hooked around my torso. I cradled her to my side with my arm, making sure she didn't touch the cold metal of the railing.

I watched her for an hour straight, seeing the face that haunted my dreams every night. Her lips parted just the way they used to, showing a small glimpse of her white teeth. Small freckles dotted her olive-toned skin. Her beautiful face, high cheekbones, and luscious lips were exactly as I remembered.

It was hard to believe she was really there.

I'd fantasized about her so many times that I wasn't sure if this was just my imagination.

But my fingers could feel her frame. My eyes could see her chest rise with every breath she took. I could feel her pulse against my skin.

She was real.

And she was mine.

I went through hell to get her, risked my neck for a man I didn't even like, and now it was all worth it.

Crow finally gave me his daughter.

There was a gentle tap on the door before Max appeared. Dressed in the same clothes as the last time I saw him, he'd obviously been at the hospital the entire time. He didn't have a single bruise anywhere that I could see, and I was grateful my closest friend didn't get hurt at my expense.

He approached the bed then looked down at Vanessa. He watched her sleep for a second before he lifted his gaze to look at me, a smile forming on his lips. It was the kind of joy that reached his eyes. Then he gave me a thumbs-up. "Happy for you."

She was as small as I remembered, fitting within the crook of my arm perfectly. Half my size but twice as aggressive, she was the perfect woman to give my heart to. "Thanks." I kept my voice low so I wouldn't wake her up. "I'm glad you're alright."

"Me?" he asked with a quiet laugh. "Not a scratch. You're the one who almost died."

"Better me than you."

His eyes narrowed on mine, a hint of affection deep within his look. "I'm glad we're both alright. The guys are fine too."

"Looks like we all got lucky."

"Extremely. What's next for you?"

"I'm not sure yet. I just want to get out of here."

"I bet. You've never been the kind of man to sit still very long."

The only reason I was still now was because of the woman in my arms. I enjoyed holding her, had missed it more than anything else.

"The boyfriend is gone?"

I shrugged. "If he's not, I'll make him gone."

"Sounds about right." He patted my shoulder. "I'm gonna take off. I'm in desperate need of a shower."

"I agree," I teased.

He patted my shoulder again, but this time a little harder to cause me pain. "I just risked my ass for you."

"And I'll risk mine for you anytime."

"Give me a call when you're feeling better. I know you won't be in the field for a while, so take your time."

I held his gaze, but I hesitated when I heard what he said. Vanessa and I had barely said a few words to each other, but we didn't need to have a long conversation to establish what we both already knew. It was her and me—forever. I couldn't risk my life for work anymore. I'd have to give it up like I did last time.

But Max assumed otherwise. "Love you, man."

"Love you too, Max." I watched my friend walk out and saw Conway step inside immediately afterward. He was on his feet and moving around, but his face was in terrible shape. Both of his eyes were swollen black and blue, and the rest of his face was discolored from the beating he took in the alleyway. He didn't walk like he normally did, with a straight back and even straighter shoulders. He had a slight rigidness, doing his best to move without inflaming whatever was broken in his body.

He stopped at my bedside and looked down at his sister. He watched her for several seconds, the teddy bear in my arms. After what seemed like an eternity, he met my gaze again. "I haven't seen my sister that happy in three months."

It was the first time I felt anything remotely close to happiness. "How are you?"

He ignored his sister and focused on me. "Alive."

"That makes two of us."

He gripped the rail that divided us, standing beside my bed just the way his father had. "My father told me everything you did. That we'd all be dead without you."

I didn't say anything, unsure what to say to a statement like that. I wasn't trying to be humble. If anything, it was awkward. Conway had been cold to me just the way his father had been, even though he was a sinner the same way I was.

"And you saved my wife…" His voice broke at the end, his emotion overriding his coolness. "If your men hadn't gotten there first…I wouldn't have been able to find her again. I wouldn't have met my future son or daughter." He broke eye contact, unable to look at me as the horrible thought crossed his mind. "I want to thank you for what you did, but I don't even know where to begin. My father and uncle mean a lot to me. But my wife…the way I feel about her… I wouldn't have been able to live with myself if I survived and she didn't."

That was the way I felt about Vanessa. I'd rather die than let something happen to her because living without her was just too damn hard.

"So, thank you."

I didn't look at him when I replied. "You're welcome, Conway."

"I misjudged you," he said quietly. "I never gave you a chance."

"Can't say that I blame you. The past sticks to you like glue sometimes. You were just looking out for your sister and your family. I respect that."

"Doesn't change the fact that I was wrong. I should have listened to my sister. She's the smartest person I know. Instead of trusting her instincts and actually listening to her, I encouraged my father to get rid of you. The past three months have been for nothing. That's time you'll never get back."

"But I have the rest of my life with her. So it was all worth it. I'd do it again in a heartbeat."

Conway pulled his hands from the rail and placed them in his pockets. "You could have died."

"Still would have done it. When I got that phone call, I didn't think about the bullshit you guys put me through. That wasn't important. I thought about how Vanessa would feel if she lost her brother and her father. I couldn't let that happen. She loves you both with all her heart, and if she loves you…then I…don't want you to die."

His eyes filled with gratitude as he dropped his aloof stance. Conway Barsetti always carried himself with ruthlessness, like he didn't care about anyone or anything. He seemed cold, untouchable. But he left all that indifference at the door and had an honest conversation with me, wearing his heart on his sleeve. "You're a better man than I am. If the situation were reversed, I don't think I would have helped you."

At least he was honest about it.

"But now, I would. Anything you ever need, I'm there. If there's anything I can ever do for you, don't hesitate to ask. You have my loyalty. I know I'll never be able to repay you for what you did for me…but I'd like to try."

Her family didn't understand that they didn't owe me anything. I didn't do it for them. I did it for her. "There is something you can do for me."

"Name it," he said immediately. "Anything you want, I can make it happen."

I let go of Vanessa and extended my arm. "Shake my hand."

A grin slowly spread across his face. "That's it?"

"That's it."

Conway beamed before he gripped my hand and shook it. "To new beginnings."

"Yes. To new beginnings."

―――――

WHEN THE DOCTORS discharged me from the hospital,

I was relieved to get out of bed and on my feet again. I didn't feel like a man lying there, helpless with tubes and wires hooked up to my body.

When both of my feet hit the tile floor, I finally stood up straight and took a deep breath. The last thing I remembered from that night was snapping someone's neck before I fell to my knees and collapsed.

Vanessa watched me warily, like I might tip over and fall once more. There was nothing she could do to catch me, not when I would crush all of her bones with my weight. "Are you alright?"

The pain was still in my shoulder, but that would be there for a while. "Yes." I took her hand in mine, feeling her warm and soft fingers. I gripped them tightly, to make sure they were real. For the last three months, all I'd been holding was booze. "Let's go."

We left the hospital room and moved into the waiting room, where her entire family was gathered. Her parents were there, along with her aunt and uncle. My favorite Barsetti was there—Carmen. Carter was there too, a man I hadn't interacted with much. They all stared at me, but this time, it wasn't with hatred and disgust.

It was with gratitude and respect.

Crow stepped forward first. "You look like you're in good shape."

"I've been shot before. No big deal." I had multiple scars on my body from all the places I'd been pierced with a bullet. My tattoo artist usually covered them up again so they weren't so visible. Now I had a new mark on my shoulder that needed to be covered once it was healed.

Crow didn't react to my words, even though anyone else would have been disturbed by that information. "Is there anything we can do for you? How about we give you a ride to your place?"

"I'll drive him," Vanessa said. "I'll be taking care of him for a while. When he's feeling better, we'll head back to Florence to see how Conway is doing."

I had the strength to make it to Florence now, and I certainly didn't need her to take care of me. But all I wanted was to be alone with her, to finally drop the walls that I projected and be open with the woman I loved. I wanted to feel her with my hands, kiss her naked body everywhere, make love to her the way I fantasized about. I just wanted my woman, my baby. I put my life on the line to save the people she loved. Now it was my turn to be rewarded. And all I wanted was this woman in my bed, buck naked with her legs spread. She was mine now. I owned her, and it was my right to enjoy her. When I was fulfilled, I would let her visit her family again.

Not a moment sooner.

Crow hugged Vanessa first and kissed her on the forehead. "See you soon, *tesoro*. Love you."

"Love you too," she whispered.

Crow moved to me next, and instead of ignoring me the way he used to, he shook my hand, looked me in the eye, and said, "Let me know if you need anything, Griffin." He placed his hand on my shoulder and gave me a gentle pat, the way he did with Conway.

Words didn't come from my throat the way I wanted them to. All I did was nod.

Pearl hugged her daughter next then came up to me. It was the first time I'd seen her since everything happened. She hadn't come into my room to visit me. Everyone watched her as she faced me, the silence surrounding us. Then, unexpectedly, she started to cry.

I'd never been comfortable around crying women, so I didn't know what to do. Vanessa hardly ever did it, thankfully. I avoided Pearl's gaze, feeling intrusive for looking at her during her despair.

Then she moved into my chest and hugged me.

Hugged me.

I'd never even gotten a handshake from anyone, let alone a hug. I stood there awkwardly as she clung to me, and it took me a few seconds to return the affection. My large arms surrounded her, feeling her petiteness.

Vanessa smiled as she watched her mother sob against me.

"You saved my son," Pearl said into my chest. "You saved my husband…my brother…my daughter. Thank you so much." She stayed in place, pouring her heart out to me.

I patted her back, still feeling ill at ease touching her like this.

"I wanted to visit you in your room, but I was still too upset…and now I'm even worse." She pulled away and looked up at me, tears streaming down her cheeks and ruining her mascara. "My family means everything to me. If I lost them…any of them…I would lose myself. Because of you, I get to sleep with my husband beside me. Thank you, Griffin. I'm so sorry for the way I—"

"I accept your apology, Mrs. Barsetti. And you're welcome." I gave her a pat on the back before I pulled away, distancing myself from her. Her emotional turmoil was more than I could stand. Vanessa spoke highly of her mother, saying she was the strongest person she'd ever met. It was unlike her to cry, so seeing the tears made the situation even more profound. "What I want more than anything is to move forward and start over."

Pearl rubbed her eyes with her fingertips, wiping away her smeared mascara in the process. "Of course. You're a very brave man, and I feel better knowing my daughter has you. I know you would do anything for her."

Those words meant a lot to me because it was all I ever wanted, to prove to her family I was the best man to take care of her. I'd said those words to her father many times, but they always bounced back at me. "I would, as I would for all of you."

The Barsettis stared back at me, all tense and touched by what I said.

"You're welcome to join us whenever you want," Pearl said. "Our home is always open to you."

It was a relief to feel welcome for once, to feel the universal acceptance of the Barsetti family. They didn't just welcome me because they had to, but because they genuinely cared for me now. I felt like a friend—for the first time. Whenever I had been at the winery or anywhere on their property, they'd constantly watched me like a hawk. I'd said a few words to Carmen, and Cane had acted like I'd tried to rape her. Now I'd finally earned the acceptance of them all…which was all I ever wanted. "Thank you, Mrs. Barsetti."

GUNS AND AMMUNITION were still on the coffee table where I'd left them. A half-drunk glass of scotch was there too, and the condensation from the liquid had made a ring on the wood because it'd been sitting there for so long. The lights were still on because I'd abandoned everything before I left to save Conway.

Vanessa stepped inside and surveyed the room, searching for the changes that had occurred over the past three months. But she wouldn't find any because nothing was different. I hadn't changed anything, not even the room where she kept her art supplies. I'd been too pathetic to throw anything away.

I came up behind her, staring at her small frame in my living room. She was in a blue summer dress, her olive skin looking delicious in the color. Her arms were by her sides, and her breathing was quiet.

I approached her slowly, my hands slightly shaking from the moment I was about to embrace. For the last three months, I had sat in this apartment alone, drinking scotch and trying to forget about the woman who made me so happy. I thought I would never see her again, let alone in this very apartment.

Now she stood in front of me, beautiful as ever.

I stopped when my chest hit her back. My hands gripped the backs of her arms, feeling the pulse under the callused pads of my fingertips. My hands constricted around her, holding her tighter than I meant to. My desperation to squeeze her came from longing, not from rage. I needed to feel her intimately to understand she was really there.

She was there with me.

I rested my forehead against the back of her head, my face surrounded by her dark hair. I recognized her scent, the same smell that smothered my sheets. It reminded me of winter, of the blissful months I'd kept her warm in that small apartment. It reminded me of the moments I tried to fight, the moments when I fell so hard for her no matter how much I worked to resist it. This woman changed me, turned me from a monster into a heartfelt man. I still had rage, but that rage now only flamed when I thought she was in danger…or when someone she loved was in danger.

She was the first person to bring me to tears, the first woman to break my heart. I remembered the sensation because it felt so strange. Every breath burned my lungs. My throat ached because it seemed like it was on fire. My eyes were coated with a sheen of moisture. It happened so fast and with such profoundness, I wasn't even sure what was happening.

Only Vanessa could bring me to my knees.

Only Vanessa could make me feel loved.

Only Vanessa could make love as hard as I fought.

Only Vanessa could bring tears to my eyes.

The sound of my own breaths was audible to my ears because they slowly increased, growing deeper and harder. I could hear hers too, listen to them rise as the intensity between us turned into a raging storm. My hands never left her arms, keeping her against me. I let my chest expand into her back, felt her push back against me as her lungs filled with air.

Her breaths reached a breaking point, and that's when she started to cry.

It was quiet, barely audible. It was only apparent because of the way her breathing turned irregular. Soon, her whimpers filled my quiet apartment. She'd never been the kind of woman to cry, not even under the threat of death, but she was coming apart—piece by piece.

My hands released her arms, and I secured my arms over her chest, my thick limbs covering her completely with the girth of two tree trunks. I pulled her against me, trapping her in place so she couldn't run.

She used to be my prisoner. And now, she was my prisoner again.

This time, she would never get away.

My hold on her was too tight. Even if she wanted to leave, I would never allow it.

She gripped my arms with her hands. "I missed you so much…" She turned her head slightly, showing me her cheek. Tears ran from her eyes all the way to her chin. Her perfect makeup started to run. "It was the hardest thing I've ever had to do. I couldn't sleep, I couldn't eat… I couldn't do anything. I didn't care about anything. Life was just…a meaningless blur. I tried to argue with my father to get him to change his mind. When it was no use, it was even more painful."

I didn't need to know how much she'd suffered. I knew this woman loved me completely, loved me for all the good and the bad. She accepted me exactly as I was, seeing the best in me during my worst times. Walking away from her was the hardest thing I've ever had to do. I never really moved on with my life because it was too difficult. She loved me the way I loved her, so she didn't need to tell me how hard the last three months had been.

I already knew.

"And now I can feel you." She gripped my arms tighter. "I can feel your strong heartbeat again. I can smell your scent. I'm standing in the very place where I saved your life. This apartment was home to me…and here I am again. It's true, but I feel like someone is going to take it away from me at any moment."

Nothing could come between us, not ever again. If someone tried to pull her away from me, I would just hold on tighter. "Never." I moved my face into her neck, feeling her thudding pulse right against my mouth. "Your family owes me for all eternity. There was only one thing I asked for, one thing they had to hand over. That prize is in my arms now. I own you more than I ever did. You're irrevocably and permanently mine. Forever." I forced my arms to relax so I wouldn't crush her under my hold. I wanted her so much that I didn't care if I hurt her a little in the process. My lips brushed against her neck then the shell of her ear. I'd kissed her in the hospital, but I didn't get to take my time, to treasure the feel of her lips. Her tears mingled with mine then, and while the moment was euphoric, I wanted more.

"I want you to own me…forever." She slowly circled in my arms, turning until she faced me, one teardrop stuck to her cheek. Her wet eyes reflected the light from the ceiling, making it seem like there were stars in her gaze. She stared up at me, her hands moving over my t-shirt as they migrated to my chest. She licked her lips, tasting the salt of her own tears.

My hands cupped her face, and I stared into her eyes, my chest rising and falling with the deep breaths I took. Her hair was caught in my fingertips, her smell mixed with mine. All I wanted to do was enjoy the happiness I'd finally earned, but I had to pause and treasure the moment. It was a moment I would never forget, a moment I would still recall as an old man.

Her hands moved over my wrists, and she gripped them, her plump lips waiting for my kiss.

I could have swept her off her feet the second we were in the door. I could have carried her to my bed and shoved myself inside her without even taking off her dress. But instead of rushing into the moment of bliss, I wanted to take my time. I wanted to make it last, to give it a chance to heal both of our broken hearts.

My forehead moved to hers, and I closed my eyes for a brief moment before I finally kissed her.

Finally enjoyed her.

The second our lips touched, I felt that old spark. I felt the heat between our mouths, the steady burn from the fire in both of our bellies. Her kiss was exactly the same as I remembered, delicious and sexy. She kissed me slowly, feeling my lips in between hers before she allowed me to grip her bottom lip between my teeth. Our breathing filled the room, evolving from emotional to desperate.

Our mouths moved faster, and I cradled her face in my hands, moving closer into her body as our passion rekindled. As if this woman had never left, my desire for her was paramount. She was my fantasy, but I didn't just want her because of the way she made me hard. I wanted her because of the way she softened my heart.

She rose on her tiptoes to kiss me more easily, so she could have more of my mouth. She gripped my shoulders for balance, and as old tears dripped down her face, I tasted the salt on my tongue.

I hadn't kissed her like this in so long.

I wasn't even sure if it was real.

My hands gripped her slender waist, and I lifted her up

effortlessly. I pulled her leg around my waist, anchoring her to me as I carried her down the hallway and to my bedroom. The pain in my shoulder didn't hurt me at all, not when my mind was focused on the beautiful woman in my arms.

My feet tapped against the hardwood floor, and our heavy breathing filled the narrow hallway. She kissed me harder as I carried her to bed, excited to feel me sink between her legs just the way I used to every single morning and night.

I moved to the bed and pressed her back into the mattress, my lips never leaving hers. I'd slept in this bed alone since she left, never having any visitors to fight the loneliness. The only company I ever had was my hand— and that wasn't as good as the real thing.

My hand moved up her dress until I touched her thong. Soft and lacy, it was just as I remembered before I even looked at them. This one was black, one of my favorite pairs. I pulled it over her luscious ass and down her gorgeous legs.

I was hard just from touching her panties, from undressing her so I could enjoy her. She was a present that I got to open, and instead of seeing the gift right away, I took my time. I pulled her dress off next, revealing more of that beautiful olive skin. Dark and unblemished, her smooth skin was sweet like honey. When I got it off, I visualized the gorgeous curves I used to enjoy every night. With perky tits, a slender stomach, and endless curves, she was exactly as I remembered. She'd lost some weight, but that didn't distract me from the obvious beauty underneath me.

My lips ached to kiss her everywhere, to pleasure my tongue with her taste. It'd been so long since I'd had a woman, since I'd been buried between a beautiful woman's legs. An eternity had passed, and looking at her tested my resolve. My mouth immediately went to the valley of her tits, and I dragged my tongue everywhere, tasting her exquisite flesh. I devoured her tits aggressively, kissing those womanly curves and sucking the nipples until they were raw.

She writhed underneath me, digging her nails through my t-shirt and moaning like she'd never been touched before. Her fingers moved into the back of my hair, and she shoved each boob into my mouth, like she couldn't get enough of me fast enough. Her excitement matched mine, and she squeezed my hips with her thighs. "Griffin…god." I wasn't even inside her yet, and she was about to come from my mouth.

My lips trailed down her stomach until I reached the apex of her thighs. With the same enthusiasm, she pulled my face between her legs and pressed into me, her head rolling back with ecstasy.

I ate her pussy with vigor, having missed her unique taste. Her arousal continued to pool between her legs, and she didn't need my wetness at all, but I wanted her anyway. I wanted to claim every inch of her, to erase anyone else she had been with since I'd been gone. I circled her clit a few times, making her spine shiver and her words emerge as a whimper. I wanted to make her come, to make her call out my name, but my cock wanted to feel her squeeze around me as she exploded.

The second my mouth was gone, she viciously yanked my shirt over my head. She clawed at it with her nails, scratching my skin in the process. She moved for my jeans next, her hands shaking in her impatience to get me naked. She finally pushed them down along with my boxers.

She stared at my cock without shame, looking at it like it was the most arousing thing she'd ever seen. She licked her lips then moaned, moaned like he was already buried inside her. "God...get inside me." She pulled me on top of her and widened her legs to give my hips the room they needed.

I knew she wanted me, but I'd never seen her look at me quite like that. After putting my weight on my hands and positioning myself against her, I pointed the swollen head of my cock at her opening and pushed.

So fucking wet.

And tight.

It was so tight I had to push slowly so I could sink inside her.

We didn't have the conversation about where we'd been and if we'd been tested. It didn't seem like it mattered right now because nothing was going to stop us from being together.

She clawed at my chest as she felt me squeeze through her soft flesh. "Yes…yes…yes." She looked up at me, her mouth open from moaning right in my face. "Jesus Christ…yes." She'd missed my cock as much as I missed giving it to her.

I kept sinking, getting reacquainted with her cunt. I didn't remember her being this tight. The first time I fucked her, it was like breaking in a virgin, but after that, her pussy formed to my cock. Now I was breaking her in all over again. That could only mean one thing.

She hadn't been fucking anyone else.

It didn't matter to me whether she had or hadn't. She'd always been mine, even if another man enjoyed her. I could make her forget he ever existed, forget his name like she didn't know it in the first place.

I kept sinking until I reached her cervix.

"Griffin." She locked her ankles together around my waist, her heels driving into my back as she tugged on me. Her nails dragged down my back, making indentations in the skin. Her lower back twitched, and her cunt squeezed me like a snake suffocating its prey. "Oh...god." She locked her gaze on mine as she came around my dick, slathering my length with her slick arousal. We weren't moving together, idle in our positions as our bodies absorbed one another. I could have started to thrust, but watching her come the second my dick was inside her was more than enough.

Her orgasm seemed to stretch on for so long. She kept clawing my back as she finished, her gorgeous face putting on a performance I would never forget. She was writhing from the pleasure of our union, just the feeling of my dick enough to make her explode.

I waited until she was done, until her screams subsided.

The pleasure slowly passed, but her eyes remained on me. She stopped carving my back with her fingernails and stared at me as she caught her breath. There was no shame in the look, no apology for hitting her threshold instead of waiting for me to join her.

And that was exactly how I liked her—unapologetic.

With my dick soaking wet, I started to thrust inside her. Through her soft flesh and slickness, my cock slid in and out. It'd been so long I forgot how incredible her pussy felt. When it was just us together, skin to skin, it was the most pleasurable experience. When we moved together like this, I couldn't just feel her tight cunt. I could feel her beating heart, her broken soul, and the endless feelings that swirled through her body. We were connected on a primal level, just man and woman. I looked into her eyes as I thrust inside her, as I made love to her at a slow and steady pace.

"Griffin." Her lips brushed against mine as she spoke, her breath heavy with arousal. "I love you…so damn much."

I didn't stop rocking, didn't stop pressing her into the mattress with my weight. My cock was harder than it'd ever been over the last three months. My hard-ons had been watered down with depression. Even the pictures I'd kept of her couldn't give me as much pleasure as she did right now. "Baby, I love you." I'd missed telling her that, missed hearing her say it to me. They were words we didn't exchange often because it seemed obvious in everything we did and said. It gave those beautiful words even more meaning.

"I miss feeling your come inside me." She grabbed my ass and pulled me harder into her, tugging on me so she could get my length deeper and deeper with each pull. She widened her legs for me, spreading them farther so she could accommodate more of my girth. "Griffin, I want it."

My hand moved into her hair, and I fisted it aggressively, yanking slightly so I could direct her gaze on me completely. I didn't sleep with anyone while she was gone because I had a ridiculous notion I might get her back. I didn't do anything because I knew it wouldn't be good like this, that the women would be nothing compared to her. If I was fucking a woman, I would picture Vanessa underneath me. I wouldn't be able to get her out of my head. If I could really pretend she was there, then the sex would be good. But no woman would ever live up to Vanessa, not in looks and not in attitude. So I tugged on her harder, dominating her and claiming her as mine. There was nothing I wanted more than to give her my come every single night, to make it stain the sheets underneath us. Her pussy was the only one I wanted to stuff.

"Come inside me," she begged, speaking against my mouth.

I hooked my arms behind her knees and bent her at a deeper angle, hitting her good and hard with every thrust. I smashed her clit and crushed the headboard, giving it to her just the way she asked. I wanted to dump my come inside my woman, but I wasn't going to cross the threshold until she came with me.

She started to claw my back again, evidence of her impending orgasm. It was her signature move in the missionary position. I knew that because I remembered everything about her, all the details that lesser men would have forgotten. I knew how to make my woman come. She moved her face into my chest and sank her teeth into my collarbone. She ignited in a blaze, screaming and clawing at the same time. She bucked against me, her pussy clenching me. She came just as hard as she had minutes ago, maybe even harder.

My dick couldn't take it anymore, and I finally exploded. The climax started from my stomach and then hit my balls. The pleasure before the explosion was so deep, so good, that I actually groaned in her face. Coming inside my woman was so much better than releasing inside a soft tissue. Her tight cunt was much better than my callused hand. My head exploded, and I dumped mounds inside her, stuffing her with more come than I'd ever produced for her. I gave it to her good and deep, all the muscles in my back tightening because it felt so right. "Jesus fucking Christ." Only one woman could make me feel this way, could make me paralyzed with pleasure. My hand still gripped her hair because I wasn't ready to let her go. I was satisfied in a way I hadn't been in months. My cock immediately started to soften after the powerful orgasm had passed, but I wasn't finished.

She wasn't finished either. She hooked her arms around my neck and locked her ankles together once more. Her lips crushed against mine as she kissed me like it was the first time all over again. "Again."

TEN

Vanessa

I came into consciousness gently, the morning light entering the room and sprinkling over my cheek and the duvet. I could feel the summer heat pierce my skin while the rest of my body was surrounded by the cool air from the central cooling system.

The sheets were soft. The pillows were softer. It was exactly as I remembered, even in my sleep. It was the place where I slept every night, and even though three months had passed, my body hadn't forgotten how wonderful this bed felt.

My eyes opened slowly, and I took in the man beside me.

Bones.

He was wide awake, his stern gaze focused on me like a gun aimed at a target. His dirty-blond hair was close to his scalp because he'd recently gotten a haircut, and the beard along his jaw was a little thicker than it had been last night. Regardless of how thick his beard was or how short his hair was, he was still the beautiful and terrifying man I'd fallen in love with.

His shoulder was still wrapped in the thick gauze, and now there was a distinct color appearing underneath the white fabric, as if he was starting to bleed through the protective covering. I sighed and stretched my body, waking up in the most peaceful way I'd ever known.

His face was close to mine, but he didn't touch me. His broad shoulders were thicker than they used to be. He hadn't put on more weight, but more muscle. In the last three months, he'd obviously pushed his workout regime.

The line around his jaw was so deep it looked like a cut from a knife. He was chiseled from stone, a statue in dedication to a god. With little to say, he was just as strong and silent as he used to be. Like no time had passed at all, everything felt the same.

Like I hadn't lost him for three months.

I tried not to think about the other women who'd been in this very bed since I'd been gone. How many had rolled around in these sheets? How many had said his name? I knew it didn't matter because none of them meant anything to him. I was the only woman he ever wanted.

Like they never happened in the first place, he'd forgotten about them by now.

I should forget them too.

I could feel his come dripping over my thighs, feel it still deep inside me. This was how I used to wake up every morning, and it was like walking into the past.

I stared at him for a while, memorizing the look of his face even though I would see it every day for the rest of my life. I wanted to soak it in, to make up for all the time we'd lost. Time had seemed to stand still since he became mine again. I'd ignored everything else in my life, from my phone to my family. Antonio had called me a few times, but I never had a chance to call him back. Now that I was with Bones again, sharing his bed and every other moment of my time, I wasn't sure when I would call him back. If I could, I would just send him a text message and say it was over between us. He'd been such a gentleman toward me, but the second I had the man I really wanted, it was like he never mattered. I felt like a horrible person for thinking that.

But it was true.

Bones continued to stare at me, hardly blinking. His muscular chest rose and fell slowly with his breathing, and the mattress slightly declined in his direction because of the weight of his frame. Instead of touching me or smothering me with kisses, he studied me like I was a picture rather than a person.

But his stare was so intimate that it felt like he was touching me everywhere.

When he spoke, his voice was deep, deeper than a bottomless pit. "Morning, baby."

I used to wear that nickname like a blanket, completely wrapped around me. It kept me warm on the frozen nights and smothered me at my loneliest times. "I love it when you call me that…I miss it."

He didn't even blink. "You'll never have to miss it again."

"I miss you right now…"

He paused, holding my gaze for a few seconds before he wrapped his thick arm around my waist and yanked me toward him. He pulled me with ease, making my tits slap against his chest before he hooked my leg over his hip. He rolled me over to my back and positioned himself on top of me, his dick already hard a while ago.

I looked at his shoulder again, seeing the color spread through the material. "You're bleeding through your bandage." I pushed him to his back and straddled his hips. His head rested on the pillow, his wide shoulders taking up most of the bed. "Let me."

His hands gripped my thighs before he squeezed my tits. "I'm fine. But my baby can ride me whenever she wants."

AFTER I CHANGED HIS GAUZE, I got into the shower. His bathroom was exactly as I remembered, from the kind of shampoo he had on the shelf and the half-used bar of soap he used every morning. He still had the same bath mat on the floor in front of the shower, and he organized his stuff on the counter the same way.

When I opened the drawer, I saw some of my old things, like my razor, toothbrush, and some eyeliner. I stared it before I shut the drawer and used his toothbrush instead. I dried my hair and slapped on some eyeliner before I put on one of his t-shirts. There were still some of my clothes here, but I preferred his.

I walked into the living room and saw him sitting on the couch in his sweatpants. Shirtless and firm, his chiseled torso led to a solid chest. He was a combination of strong muscles, all interlocking together to form a wall that couldn't be conquered. He had a cup of coffee in front of him with the news on.

It seemed like a normal day. It didn't seem like three months had come and gone without speaking. It was like that horrible event in our lives had never occurred. Neither one of us had changed at all.

He took a sip before he addressed me, his eyes on the TV. "Your phone keeps ringing."

"My phone?" I couldn't remember where I left it. After I walked into his apartment, I abandoned everything else. All I cared about was being with him, reuniting our bodies as well as our souls. I hadn't gotten laid in so long that the second his fat dick was inside me, I came so violently that the muscles in my back started to spasm. I was still sore, especially after I rode his big cock for forty-five minutes.

He nodded to the small purse I tossed on the ground last night, but he still didn't look at me.

I picked up my purse and fished through my bag until I found my phone. There were a few text messages from my mom, letting me know they got home safely with Conway. But there were also a few messages from Antonio, along with missed phone calls. He was worried about me, and I couldn't wait a few days to call him. I had to do this now. "I've got to make a phone call."

Bones kept his eyes on the TV even though I'd never seen him watch the news. He only gave a slight nod in acknowledgment.

I knew he wasn't a talkative guy, but he always looked at me, at least. He definitely knew what this was about, whether he'd looked at my phone or just had a good guess.

Shit.

Conway told Bones I had been seeing someone, so he

knew about it. But it was strange to call Antonio when I was in his house. I moved down the hallway and entered my old art room, expecting it to be empty.

But it was exactly as I'd left it.

The last painting I'd been working on was still there, half completed.

He'd kept everything.

I'd expected him to toss everything once our relationship was over. Bones wasn't a sentimental guy. He didn't wear his heart on his sleeve because he didn't even have a heart most of the time. But he kept this room, either because he couldn't handle tossing everything in the garbage or because he thought I might come back someday.

I steadied my nerves before I made the call.

Antonio answered immediately. "Thank god. I've been calling you like crazy. I saw on the news that your brother got mugged by some thugs and he was in the hospital. You haven't been home or to your gallery so I assumed you were in Milan, but I couldn't leave the office. Just wanted to see if you were okay." The sincere concern in his voice only made me feel worse about the situation.

"I'm sorry I didn't call you sooner. Everything happened so fast, and then we were at the hospital… It was a nightmare."

"Is he gonna be alright?"

"Yeah. He's got some broken ribs and his face was beat up, but he'll be alright."

"Oh, that's good to hear," he said, breathing a sigh of relief. "And you're alright too?"

I'm more than alright. I'm better than I've ever been. I lost my happiness and found it again. Ever since Bones came back into my life, I hadn't thought of Antonio once. He became an afterthought, hardly a memory. "I'm alright. And relieved."

"Me too," he said. "I'm sorry to blow up your phone, but I was just worried."

"Don't apologize. Thanks for checking in."

"So…when are you going to be home? I miss you."

Like I was punched in the face, I felt everything inside me shatter. His words knocked me out, pushed all the air from my lungs. I couldn't say it back, not even to make him feel better. It would be wrong, a betrayal to the man I was with. And it just would give Antonio false hope. "Listen…" I told him everything that had happened, but a censored version so he didn't know about the criminal pasts of my family and Bones. "We're back together now. I don't want to hurt you, Antonio, but I don't want to sugarcoat it and make it seem like there's still a chance for the two of us."

Antonio was quiet for a long time, digesting the blow slowly. He had just received a lot of information in very little time. He'd been blindsided, and I didn't blame him for being overwhelmed.

"I'm sorry…"

He sighed into the phone but still didn't say anything.

"Antonio—"

"I understand, Vanessa. You can't choose who you love. Sometimes, it's beyond our logical control. But I really think there's something here between us. The way we bought each other's paintings…the way we connect. I'm not upset about losing a woman to another man. But I am upset about losing you…because I think we have something special, something you don't have with this other man."

"I know…but I love him. We have nothing in common. Our relationship has been nothing but work. He's stubborn and hostile most of the time. But…I love him so much. If I'd met you first, I'm sure we would have been happy together and gotten married. But…I fell in love with this man, and our love is so deep I'll never shake it."

Antonio was quiet again, accepting the second blow with silence. "Then there's nothing left to say."

"Yeah…"

"Good luck, Vanessa."

"You too…" I wanted to say more, to end our final conversation on a better note. Antonio was a good man and didn't deserve this heartbreak. But if I didn't make it straightforward and cold, it would only be harder for him.

Click.

I lowered the phone and stared out the window, the guilt rising in my chest. For a moment, I really had felt something for Antonio. I felt that rush of new love; I felt that hope of a future. When he touched my hand, I felt the electricity. When he pressed his forehead to mine, I felt that hot connection between us.

But once Bones was back…it all meant nothing.

Bones triumphed over any man, every man.

I waited a few minutes before I returned to the living room. Bones was exactly where I left him, his coffee mug a little emptier from drinking. He leaned back against the couch, his stomach tight no matter what position he took. One arm hung over the back of the couch.

I stared at him for a while, waiting for him to look at me in return. The awkwardness was heavy since we both knew exactly what I'd just done. If someone else called me, I would have that conversation right in front of him. I'd never walked away to speak to someone before.

He finally turned to meet my eyes, his deep blue eyes

gazing into mine. He didn't ask me a single question or accuse me of anything. After several heartbeats, he looked away.

I considered telling him everything that had happened with Antonio, but I didn't want to listen to him tell me about his conquests over the last three months. There must have been more women than I could count on two hands. "He wanted to check on me. I ended things." It would be unfair for Bones to be angry at me, but I stayed rooted to the spot, feeling obligated to explain the situation. "I don't want you—"

Bones rose to his feet abruptly, over six feet of power. He moved toward me, his bare feet hitting the hardwood floor beneath. With broad shoulders and a narrow waist, he was a perfect triangle. His biceps were bigger than my head. He could probably crush a whole watermelon between his two palms.

My lips stopped moving when he loomed over me like that, full of hostility.

He regarded me coldly, his head slightly turned. "I'll make you forget he ever existed." He grabbed the back of my neck and looked into my face, possessing me aggressively just the way he used to. He controlled my entire body, holding on to my hair to keep me rigid. He had the power to control my breathing, to even control my heartbeat.

"You already have."

His eyes narrowed but softened at the same time. "Boys don't count. They never count." He finally released me and turned his back to me to walk into the kitchen. All the muscles of his back shifted under the skin as he carried himself.

"I didn't sleep with him."

He stopped walking but didn't turn around.

"I didn't even kiss him…"

His arms hung by his sides, and his breathing increased slightly. Just when enough silence passed that it felt like an eternity, he moved forward again—dismissing the conversation like it never happened to begin with.

HE DUG his large fingers into my ass cheeks, moving my lower body and tilting my hips to take in his length exactly the way he liked. He sat upright against his wooden headboard, his intense eyes focused on my lips. He watched me move forward and back, my tits shaking with the movements. He clenched his jaw and breathed deeply, his fingers squeezing my ass every time I took all of his length.

His eyes moved up to mine again, a hostile look of love

on his face. Sometimes when he looked at me, it was an expression that stretched between love and hate. But that was the way he expressed himself. His feelings for me were so profound, but they hovered between the two extremes.

I was careful not to touch his shoulder, to only grip his right one and hold on to his chest when I needed something for balance. But I couldn't stop myself from riding him every chance I got, making up for all the nights I slept alone. I didn't just want sex. I wanted him, and I wasn't ashamed to feel that way. Bones gave me such good sex. Whether it was his size, his confidence, or just the way he looked at me, I didn't know. No other man could make me feel the way he did.

He pressed his face close to mine and groaned from deep in his throat, his large dick throbbing inside me. He'd already made me come from grinding his pelvic bone against my clit, from giving me that predatory look that made me turn into prey. Now he was going to make me come again, to make good on his word to make me forget Antonio ever existed.

Even though he'd already accomplished that.

His hand moved to my lower back, and he pressed against me, getting me to grind against him harder. He teased me with his lips, brushing his hard jaw against me, turning me on with a kiss he never gave me. "In ten seconds, you're going to come all over me, baby. Because I said so."

I kept riding his length, pushing myself down until I was sitting on his balls. I pressed my hands against his chest, my hips starting to buck harder because his dick felt so good. His authoritative confidence turned me on, the way he commanded me with such ease. He was a man of few words because he made every single word count.

He bored his gaze into mine, his pretty eyes a contradiction to the ferocity in his gaze. "Nine."

My nipples hardened when the countdown began. Knowing there would be an explosion in so little time made my body prepare for it. Bones was so confident that he could make it happen, and that confidence made me melt right on top of him.

"Eight." He squeezed my right cheek before he gave it a hard slap.

I shivered at the hit, my body shifting forward.

"Seven." He gripped my right tit, squeezing it hard before he flicked his thumb over my nipple. "Six." He dragged his fingers down the valley of my breasts, picking up the sweat my body produced, and slowly glided them down to my belly button. "Five."

My pussy was already starting to tighten.

He kept his eyes on me, not needing to watch his movements. "Four." His fingers reached my clit, rubbing it gently the second he felt my wet folds.

I shivered, my nails clawing into his chest. My hips didn't move as fast because there was overwhelming stimulation in so many places.

He pressed his face close to mine as his fingers kept working my clit. "Three." His soft lips were on mine, and he kissed me, controlling my mouth while his fingers played me like a violin. He breathed into my lungs and then pulled my bottom lip between his teeth. He gave a slight nibble before he released them. "Two."

"Griffin—"

"I haven't said one yet." He circled my clit hard, his fingers getting wet from my opening. His lips were nearly on mine, but he didn't kiss me. He looked into my eyes, watching me come apart just the way he orchestrated.

My nails cut into him deeper because I could feel the explosion knocking on the gates. I hadn't felt this full in months, hadn't had his enormous cock inside me like this in a lifetime. It was the womanliest sensation I'd ever felt —to have this man buried within me. He loved me, loved me with just his look. He didn't say it often because he didn't need to. He showed me every day just the way he was showing me now. He didn't care about Antonio or any other man I spent time with. They were nothing compared to him—and he knew it. "One…"

"No." I stopped rocking, so he guided me up and down while his fingers rubbed me harder. "I control the clock, not you."

"Griffin…" My plea died in my mouth, the rest escaping as a whisper.

He kissed me again, this time giving me his tongue. His mouth took over mine, conquering it like a king seizing a new country. He had all of me, and he knew it. I was the puppet, and he was the master. His tongue pulled away, and he breathed into me, his kiss turning idle.

I knew his permission was coming…it was almost there.

"One."

"Thank god." Obediently, my cunt clenched around him as the inferno began. I was burned by his fire and turned into hot ash. The sensation heightened my release, made me feel instead of think. Screams, moans, and incoherent words flew out of my mouth. It was the most euphoric high he'd ever given me. It was spiritual, carnal. "You're one hell of a man…" I pressed my forehead against his with my eyes closed, sweat dripping down my back and in between my cheeks. It was so good, and as it passed, the memory of the sensation was still profoundly vivid.

When I opened my eyes again, I found him staring at me.

Staring at me with a whole new expression. It was different from any I'd ever seen, more aggressive than all the others combined. "I'm your man."

I LAY IN BED, lost in a dream with Bones beside me. It was sometime in the middle of the night, when the city was asleep under the stars. The summer heat couldn't penetrate these walls because Bones liked it cold as ice in the apartment.

I dreamed that nothing had changed, that I was alone in my new apartment in Florence. I slept in my bed alone, the sheets frozen without Bones beside me. All the anguish from his disappearance acted as an anchor on my chest, weighing me down to the bottom of the ocean. It felt so real, like I'd lost him again. Hot tears burned up my throat, and my eyes smoldered with emotion.

My hand reached out across the bed, searching for the man of steel beside me. My hand hit the rock-hard block that I recognized as his chest. My eyes opened, and I saw him beside me, exactly where I left him.

Panic still burned through my veins, as if seeing him and touching him weren't enough. The memory of my lonely night was still vivid. Touching him, feeling him, making love to him wasn't enough to wipe my memories away.

I gulped in a huge breath of air and finally fed my lungs oxygen.

Bones stirred at my touch then propped himself up on his elbow, his silhouette outlined like hard stone. He looked down at me, his expression visible in the darkness. Despite his sleepiness, he didn't appear frustrated by the disturbance. "Baby, I'm here." He moved my hand over his heart, allowing me to feel that profound thump deep inside his chest, the cadence of his life.

I felt the heartbeat against my palm, felt the strength circulate through his body. "How did you…?"

"Because I have the same nightmare every night." He brought my palm to his lips and kissed the center, where my web of lines started. "That's when I pull you closer, so I know this is real."

I moved closer to him and hooked my leg over his waist, feeling his hot skin against my thigh. My arm circled his muscular torso, and instead of hugging a teddy bear, it seemed like I was hugging a large piece of rock. My face rested against his sternum, where I could still feel his heartbeat.

He got comfortable beside me and ran his fingers through my hair. For a monster, he could touch me so delicately. He knew how to restrain his strength so he could caress me instead of injure me. He had the softest touch I'd ever known—and the softest kiss.

I couldn't go back to sleep, not when the dream still haunted me. When he left, I found myself in a dark pit I never thought I could crawl out of. The memory of that feeling reminded me how bad it was…not that I'd forgotten. I never wanted to feel that way again. I didn't want to be alone like that, to wonder what he was doing and if he was thinking about me. Sleep eluded me, so I lay against him, telling myself that the nightmare was over for good.

Bones didn't go back to sleep either. His breaths never deepened, and his hand continued to move through my hair.

I positioned myself so I could face him, my head on the pillow beside his.

His hand moved down my chest and to my stomach, where he palmed my belly with his large fingers. He could span my entire stomach with just his hand, his fingers touching both my rib cage and my hip.

I'd always been a petite woman, but I felt tiny in comparison to him. He could kill me with one hand, could crush me with those powerful hands. I watched the light from outside reflect in his eyes as he stared at me. At this time of night, his eyes didn't look blue. They looked black instead. His jaw was hard as ever, casting a shadow even though it was dark in the room. The hair along his jaw was starting to grow thicker since he hadn't shaved since we'd arrived at the apartment. Most of our time had been spent in bed, our bodies getting reacquainted with one another. None of my family members had called me, and I was grateful because I didn't feel like talking to them right now.

My hand moved up his shoulder to the edge of the gauze that covered his wound. "How is it?"

His callused fingertips continued to rub against my soft skin. "Fine." He hardly moved his mouth when he spoke, his words always clipped and to the point. He'd never said much before, but now he said even less. Just being together was enough conversation for him.

He'd been shot before, but he'd never been as crippled as he was after this attack. The bullet must have hit him a different way this time, caused enough damage to make him pass out from the loss of blood. "Even if it weren't fine, you wouldn't tell me, would you?"

His expression didn't change.

"I'll take that as a no." My hand moved back to his chest, where I explored the muscles of his abdomen and torso. I stared at his masculine jawline, the way it was chiseled like the different layers of the Grand Canyon. There were so many small details I'd missed about him, from the look of his jaw to the feel of his powerful muscles under my fingertips. I'd missed his big heart, his coldness, and most of all, I missed the way he could stare at me like that. Minutes would pass without a single blink, and he would still seem just as interested in me as he was an hour ago. Only a powerful man could hold eye contact with someone like that without bowing down from the hostility. He'd never been afraid of anyone, not even my father and uncle. "I've never been so low in my life." My eyes shifted away from his, unable to look at him as I spoke. "I've never known that kind of sorrow. Those three months were just…unbearable. I hardly slept. I hardly ate. I spent the first few weeks crying more than I ever have in my life. It was such a dark time for me. Anytime something bad has happened to me, I've always been resilient. I never shed a single tear. But this time, it was too much for me. I didn't speak to my father for a long time. I couldn't stand even looking at him. I was distant from everyone. Even when they tried to check on me, I didn't want to see them. My artwork changed. It wasn't full of vibrant colors and glorious landscapes. It was full of you, cast in dark shadows. I lost who I was…because I didn't know who I was without you." I'd always found solace when I looked into his powerful gaze, but now I wasn't sure if I could look him in the eye. I'd confessed my deepest depression, and a part of me was ashamed it was so bad. I'd been raised to be a strong woman, had always considered myself to be one, but when I lost the love of my life…I lost myself too. When he said nothing in return, I lifted my gaze to look at him again.

His hand slid up my neck then cupped my cheek. "When

I found out about the hit, I didn't tell your father as a ploy to get you back. I didn't join the fight because I thought it would lead to redemption in your father's eyes. Max told me it wasn't my problem, that the Barsettis had insulted me too many times and destroyed my life. They didn't deserve my help. They took away the one thing that mattered to me. If I let them die, then I would have a better chance of getting you back since they'd be out of the way."

I didn't even want to think about that outcome. The idea of losing all the people I loved destroyed me. My family was everything to me, and without them, I wouldn't even know what it meant to be a Barsetti.

"But I didn't think about any of those things. Your family meant everything to you, even more than I did. If you lost them, you would never be the same. You would never recover from the despair. It would consume you, diminish your light forever, and turn you into a different person. That was all I cared about, not whether they lived or died. Your family had never been anything but cruel to me, but that was irrelevant at the time. I stepped in for you—and for no other reason."

I felt the distant ache in my chest, the warning of impending tears.

"The past three months are a blur to me. I spent most of it drunk or working. I'd always been a depressed man, but I took it to a whole new level."

I was relieved he didn't talk about the women he brought here, the meaningless fucks that made him feel even more empty.

"My bitterness rose as my intoxication increased. I hated your family in a whole new way, the way they judged me for the same sins they committed. I understood they were trying to protect the one innocent person in their family, but I thought it was bullshit all the same. But when I knew they were all going to die…I had to do something. Because no matter how much time had passed, it didn't change my feelings for you. The alcohol and the depression couldn't wipe away the holy memory I had of you. You were the one good thing in my life, the one thing that turned me from a monster into a man. I took a bullet for your father—but I really took it for you."

Tears leaked from my eyes and fell directly onto the pillow. All that time apart had been torture for both of us, and also needless. We should have been together in the first place. We should always have been together.

"The pain you felt…I felt it too." He spoke of a horrible past but with no emotional response. He said it simply, not with the bitterness he previously described. "My life had been empty before, but it never felt hollow. Once you were gone, I didn't know how to go back to that way of living. I only killed for money, but that didn't give me any enjoyment anymore. Everything became meaningless." His thumb wiped away a tear, letting it soak into his callused skin. The day he left, he'd battled his own tears. And when I was back in his arms, he showed the same emotion I'd probably never see again. This emotional behemoth had been moved to tears only twice—and probably never before that. "Your father said he would do anything for me, give me anything I asked for. There was only one thing I wanted." He wiped away the other tear. "You know exactly what that was. But what you don't understand is how I meant it."

"Then how did you mean it?" I whispered.

His fingers moved under my chin, keeping my eyes directed on him. "That you're mine."

"I am yours… I've always wanted to be yours."

"No. You aren't my baby, my woman. You're my personal property. You're a gift given to me from my enemy. That means I'll never let you go. You have no voice or choice in the matter. If you ever want to leave me, you can't. If you ever fall in love with someone else, I'll kill him. You're my property, baby. That's the price you'll pay for the sacrifice I made." Like the monster he used to be, he claimed me as a prize and vowed he would never let me go. I was his prisoner all over his again, just as I was when we tried futilely not to fall in love. "My words aren't romantic. They're barbaric. But I don't care. That's the price your family has to pay for what they've done to me, for how much they've made me suffer. And baby, if that disappoints you, I really don't care." His hand moved to my neck, his fingers gently squeezing me.

If a man had said something like that to me a year ago, I would have slapped him across the face. But with Bones, I loved him for exactly who he was, even when he was being brutal. "I don't want to go anywhere, Griffin. So I'll gladly be your prisoner…this time."

His fingers gently squeezed me again. "I'm glad we have an understanding. You're sexy when you fight, but you're sexier when you give in to me."

"I'm not giving in to you," I said. "Not when it's exactly what I want."

His hand moved to the back of my head, digging into my hair. He gently tugged on it and brushed his lips past mine. He didn't kiss me, purposely teasing me. "Good answer, baby." He positioned himself on top of me then closed his mouth around mine.

He needed to rest his shoulder, so I should push him to his back and straddle his hips, but when I felt his weight sink me into the mattress along with this big dick, the thought left my mind. Now all I wanted was him inside me, to feel him conquer me the way he promised.

He locked my knees back with his arms then slid inside me, moaning as he felt me. "Mine." He rocked into me hard, hitting me at a punishing pace right from the beginning. "And you will always be mine."

HE FUCKED me first thing in the morning. Didn't even wait for me to wake up first.

He moved me to my back, separated my thighs, and pounded into me. He pinned me down so I wouldn't move and coated my body with this sweat. He ground hard and fast, pushing me to a climax so he could quickly follow. Then he got off me and walked into the shower like nothing happened.

Like I wasn't just stuffed with all of his come.

I went back to his sleep with his seed inside me, and when I woke up hours later, Bones wasn't in the bedroom.

I pulled on his t-shirt and walked into the living room, expecting to see him sitting on the couch with a scotch on the table.

My prediction was right, but he wasn't alone. Max was there too.

Max sat on the couch beside him and examined his shoulder. His scotch was on the table, and he was dressed in jeans and a black t-shirt. He didn't have ink the way Bones did. His tanned skin was untouched. "I sent Shane into the field. He'll be alright. You should be good as new in a month, so you'll start your rotation then." Max released his arm and stopped staring at the white bandage that covered Bones's shoulder.

"Max." Bones's deep voice vibrated with tension, like whatever he was going to say next wouldn't be pleasant. "You know I can't be involved anymore. I didn't think we even needed to have this conversation."

I stopped before the kitchen table, unsure if I should be listening to this.

Max's nostrils flared in fury, just the way Bones's did when he was really ticked about something. "You're kidding me, right?"

Bones turned his way, his entire body rigid with aggression. "Do I ever kid?"

"The only reason you quit the first time was because her father made you. News flash, you don't owe that asshole anything anymore." He rested his forearms on his knees, so absorbed in his conversation with Bones that he didn't notice me in the background.

"First of all, no one makes me do anything." Bones grabbed his glass and downed the entire contents with one gulp. "And secondly, don't call him that."

Max's eyes widened to the size of baseballs. "You're defending him?"

"No. Just don't call him that." He grabbed the second glass of scotch and drank that too. "He's still Vanessa's father, so out of her respect for her, keep your comments to yourself."

Max rolled his eyes. "I put my ass on the line to save those guys. We all did."

"No, we did it for Vanessa."

"Whatever," he snapped. "I risked my neck for those assholes that called you trash. And now you're going to bail on me?" He pressed his hands against his chest, expressing his disappointment. Then he dropped his arms, his shoulders sagging with defeat. "You can't do that. We're a foursome. We need four."

"You can replace me. Any guy would want the job."

"But I don't trust any guy. You can't turn your back on us."

Bones massaged his knuckles, his breathing increasing along with his anger. "I'm not turning my back on you. If you ever need something, I'm there. I'd risk my life to save someone you love—in a heartbeat. But that's not what you're asking me. You're asking me to keep killing people for cash."

"And you like killing people, and you like cash." Max stared at his friend in disbelief, looking at Bones in a way I'd never seen him. "Come on, man. Don't let her tell you what to do."

"She didn't ask me." He brought his voice down, prob- ably worried about waking me up. "She's never asked me.

And Crow wouldn't ask me either, not after what I did for him. This is voluntary. This is what I want."

"To do what?" he asked incredulously. "What are you going to do? Sit on your ass and get fat?"

Bones didn't rise to the insult. Max seemed to be the only person who could speak his mind around him. "Look what happened to Conway. He got mixed up with the wrong people. They didn't just come after him, but his pregnant wife too. I have no problem risking my life every day, no matter the odds. But I can't risk Vanessa." He shifted his gaze to the ground. "I just can't…" His voice trailed away, pregnant with the emotion he didn't express.

Max turned away, his shoulders still slumped with disappointment.

"Every time I leave, it kills her." Bones continued on, his voice quieter than before. "I can't keep doing that to her, especially when I don't need the money. I've lived my life without her…and we both know how that turned out."

Max turned his gaze back to Bones, and there was a look of sympathy.

I wondered what he was referring to.

"Think about it for a little while," Max said. "Even if you decide to leave, I need you for a few more things. You can't bail before then."

After a long pause, Bones finally nodded in agreement. "That's fine."

Max patted him on the back. "How's the pain?"

"There is no pain."

He nodded to Bones's shoulder. "I meant the gunshot wound."

"Like I said, no pain."

Max gave him an incredulous look, like he couldn't believe a word he said. "It's okay to feel pain, man. I know you've been shot a lot, but it's normal for it to hurt like a bitch."

He shook his head slightly. "Vanessa is my painkiller. And she's potent."

AFTER MAX LEFT, I returned to the living room, pretending I just woke up.

Bones was on the couch, a bottle of scotch sitting next to his glass. His knees were wide apart, and his chiseled torso still looked tight even when he was relaxed. He turned his head slightly my way, barely greeting me. "How'd you sleep?"

"Fine. Until you fucked me until I woke up."

He turned back to the TV. "Are you complaining?"

I crossed my arms over my chest and regarded him, just wearing one of his big t-shirts. "No. And I slept well when I went back to sleep the second time."

"Are you disappointed I didn't wake you up the same way?" He turned to me, the corner of his mouth raised in a smile. His arrogance was the same as it'd always been. He loved to be a smartass, to get a rise out of me whenever possible.

I looked at the bottle of scotch on the table. "You're drinking too much."

"No, I'm not."

"It's eleven in the morning."

"And I usually start drinking at nine. So there's been an improvement."

I walked to the coffee table and grabbed the half-empty bottle. "I don't care about your drinking. But you're still on medication, so you shouldn't be drinking alcohol at all."

"I've been shot at thirteen times before this." He turned his gaze back to the TV. "And I was never on medication any other time. So, trust me, the scotch is fine."

"No, it's not." I confiscated the bottle and the glass and carried it back to the kitchen.

He didn't turn around to look at me.

"No more drinking for a few weeks."

He still didn't make a protest.

I walked back to the couch, suspicious of his silence. I stopped at his knee and stared down at him, his t-shirt as big as a blanket around my slender body.

After a minute of silence, he grabbed my wrist and tugged me into his lap. He pulled my leg over his waist and forced me to straddle him. When he pressed his hips upward, I could feel the definition of his big cock against me.

"I thought you were mad at me, not turned on."

"Who says I'm not?" His hand moved into the back of my hair, and he fisted it, getting the perfect grip so I couldn't get away. "When I've been most furious with you is when I've wanted you the most." He pressed his face close to mine, his other hand pressing on my lower back so he could force my clit against his shaft. "I'm sure you can think of when…"

When I shot him in the snow.

"I'll drink when I feel like drinking. You can put my booze away, but that won't stop me. I'll fuck you exactly when I feel like it, even if you're asleep. I will do as I damn well please—so don't waste your time."

I cocked my head to the side, challenging him with my narrowed eyes. "Really?"

He rubbed his nose against mine. "Really."

"I'm supposed to be the one to take care of you. He said no booze—so no booze."

"Trust me, I can handle it."

"You only *think* you can handle it."

He tugged on my hair, gaining dominance. "I know exactly what I can handle, baby. A few glasses a day is nothing compared to how much I used to drink when you were gone. I know my limits because I've broken my limits. I learned the consequences of my actions the hard way…so let it go."

My hands glided down his chest as my eyes remained focused on his. I thought about his conversation with Max and the subtle words they shared. Something told me they were related. "What happened?"

He stared at me, his eyes stubborn. "Doesn't matter."

"It matters to me."

He pressed a kiss to the corner of my mouth then along my jawline. Slowly, he moved, brushing past my ear and then down my neck. His kisses turned more aggressive once he reached the hollow of my throat. He swiped his tongue across my skin as he fisted my hair harder. He distracted me with his embrace—and I wasn't ashamed to admit it worked. "I think your pussy needs more come."

"You're right," I said as I let the passion sweep me off my feet. "I think she does."

WE ENDED up in bed again, lying together with the sheets bunched around our waists. Bones would slide his fingers through my hair and kiss me for no reason at all. His embraces would be slow and passionate, full of lust and love. Then he would pull away to watch me, to observe me with his perpetually intense expression.

My fingers gently rubbed over the gauze on his shoulder. "Promise me you won't drink until this is gone." It wasn't a question, so I didn't phrase it like one. I just wanted him to get better, to make sure nothing got in the way of the healing process. He was still as strong as he was before, but if he didn't take the time to slow down, his body would struggle to get better. I never asked Bones for anything because I knew he wasn't the kind of man to be bossed around, even if he was pussy-whipped.

His eyes shifted slightly back and forth as he stared into my eyes.

"You said I was a potent painkiller. So why do you need to drink anyway?" My fingers explored his collarbone and the muscles of his chest. I loved his size and strength, the way he could crush anything with his bare hands.

His eyes narrowed. "You were listening."

I didn't realize the way I'd incriminated myself, not until after the words were out of my mouth and into the world. But it was such a sweet thing for him to say that I didn't care if he knew I overheard it all. "Yes."

"Then you heard everything Max said about work."

"Yes." I continued to massage him, to feel his tight muscles with my fingertips.

"What is your opinion about it?"

"You already know what it is." My palm cupped his cheek. "I just got you back. I can't lose you again…not ever." I wanted to spend the rest of my life with this man, every single morning and every single night. "I always knew I wanted to get married and spend my life with one person. When I was younger, I dated different guys who were wrong for me, and that made me realize how much I wanted to fall in love with one man. I'm not ashamed to say I want to go to sleep with the same man every single night for the rest of my life. And I'm not ashamed to say that man is you. I never want to feel you slip through my fingers again. I never want to sleep alone ever again. I never want anything to come between us…especially not death. I want us to have a boring, quiet life, the kind of life that my father loves."

He listened to every word I said, his expression just as stern as it usually was. "I can't leave Max high and dry. I have to finish a few things first."

I wanted him never to go back into the field. I wanted it to be over for good, but after what his friends did for my family, I wouldn't be selfish and ask something like that. "I understand."

"But once that's over…I'll leave."

The chains around my chest finally came free, and the relief washed over my body. Soon enough, I wouldn't have to worry about anyone trying to hurt him ever again. We would both make an honest living in Florence, blending in with the rest of the crowd like nobodies. "Thank you."

"I'll have to find something else to do. Not sure what that is yet."

"You can help me with the gallery."

He shook his head. "That's your thing, baby. I need something of my own."

"Something safe, I hope."

The corner of his mouth rose in a smile. "Not that safe. Don't want it to be boring."

I knew he was kidding, so I let the comment go unchallenged. "So, what do we do now?"

He turned on his back and faced the ceiling, his hard body slowly rising and falling with his breaths. "I was planning on selling this place."

"Are you sure about that?"

He stared at the ceiling and gave a slight nod. "I have no use for it anymore. If we're in Florence, we'll almost never be here. And all of your family lives in Florence now, except for Carter."

"Yeah…but we should keep the house in Lake Garda."

He turned his head toward me. "You like that place?"

"Yeah. We could spend some of the winter there." We could lie by the fire, watch the snow fall outside, and stay bundled up against the cold outside the large mansion in the middle of the mountains. Being that isolated wasn't my preference, but I knew this relationship would come with compromises.

"I'd like that."

"My apartment in Florence is fine. I'm not sure if we need more space."

"No, we'll need a bigger place. I need more space."

"For what?" I asked playfully. "We're always tangled up together."

"Gym. Guns. Gin."

I chuckled. "Yeah, we'll definitely need a bigger place then. But for now, it's nice." I moved against him and tucked my leg in between his with my torso across his waist.

He turned toward me and brushed his lips against my hairline, his scruff rough against my soft skin.

"You think you can make the trip tomorrow?"

"Baby, I've been fine since the day I left the hospital. I didn't tell you otherwise because I wanted to lock you up in my prison once again."

"The front door is unlocked."

"I never locked the door when you were my prisoner before. Never needed to." He brushed his lips against my forehead. "My hands on your body were the chains that kept you bound to me—and they still keep you bound to me."

MAX STEPPED out of the elevator with his sleeves rolled up. "I fit most of it into the truck. Anything else?"

"He's just packing a few more guns." I rolled my eyes. "It's like he's preparing for war."

"For men like us, we never know when the next war is gonna

happen until it's at our doorstep. Better to be prepared."
Max had come over to help us load everything into the new
truck. Bones claimed he could do everything on his own, but
I wouldn't allow him. His shoulder was healing, and I didn't
want him to tear the ripped flesh even more.

Max crossed his arms over his chest then peered down the
hallway. "His woman packs lighter than him. Pathetic, if
you ask me."

"Yeah, but I only pack sundresses and art supplies. He
packs bullets."

He grinned. "True."

I'd never thanked Max for what he did for my family, so
now was the perfect opportunity. "Thanks for helping
Conway. It really means a lot to me."

He quickly dropped his gaze, the intimacy of the conversation unappealing to him. "You mean the world to
him…so you mean the world to us."

"That's nice of you to say. If there's ever anything I can
do for you—"

He raised his palm to silence me. "You don't owe me
anything, sweetheart." He lowered his hand and placed it
in the pocket of his jeans. He glanced down the hallway
again. "Hurry the hell up, asshole. You think I don't have
other things to do?"

Bones yelled back down the hallway, his voice shaking the walls. "Shut the hell up, asshole. And no, I don't."

Max turned to me and rolled his eyes. "I've saved his life twice, and this is what I get?"

"He's a bit stubborn," I said with a smile.

He arched an eyebrow.

"Alright, he's really stubborn."

"That's more like it." He glanced at the shiny watch on his wrist before he looked at me again. "Florence, huh?"

"Yeah. I think we're going to be spending most of our time there." I was certain Max wasn't happy about that, having his closest friend five hours away.

"I'm relieved that Bones is back to normal. I didn't like the way he was before…he didn't either." The melancholy in Max's voice reached my ears. He spoke quietly, so Bones couldn't overhear our conversation. "He's happy, and I prefer him when he's happy."

It would be wrong for me to pry into Bones's life through his friend, but Bones was purposely keeping me in the dark about what happened in the last three months. "Bones said he broke his limit when it came to booze and he learned his lesson the hard way… What happened?"

Hesitation was in Max's eyes when he looked at me. "He didn't tell you?"

"No. He wants to keep it from me, which is unlike him. He usually tells me everything."

"I think he's embarrassed."

"Bones?" I asked incredulously. "He's never embarrassed."

"Maybe ashamed is the better word, then."

I stepped closer to him so we could share whispered secrets. "What happened, Max?"

He looked down the hallway again, to check if Bones was coming. "The only reason I'm telling you is because I want you to understand how low this guy was. He didn't brush off your breakup like it never happened. So when you go back to your family, you better make sure he's receiving every bit of respect he deserves."

"Of course." I would never allow my family to call him trash ever again.

"When you left, he stayed home and avoided everyone. He never went out. He drank a lot. About a month after you broke up, his drinking got worse. He was on the verge of alcohol poisoning when he crashed his truck into a pole. He was taken to the hospital and treated. He was banged up, but also lucky."

My hand immediately flew into my hair then slid down my neck. I massaged the tense muscles along the back of my neck, feeling the kinks of stress. A gasp escaped under my breath, and my chest ached as I tried to breathe. "No…"

"He got clean for a while, until he was able to trust himself again. But those three months were really difficult for him. He worked a lot because that was the only thing that could take his mind off you. But he wasn't working, he was drinking. Women weren't around, so he didn't have that as a distraction."

I'd pictured Bones with all the women who'd slept in his bed after I left. When I'd touched the sheets, a part of me wondered how many women had been in that exact spot. I'd tried not to focus on it, knowing Bones had every right to do whatever he wanted, but it killed me all the same. Hearing this revelation chased away the acid that burned in my stomach. "What do you mean, women weren't around?"

"I mean it exactly as it sounds," he said. "He wasn't with anyone when you were apart."

I couldn't wipe the surprise from my face. So much relief washed through me, like a river cleansing my veins.

"He didn't tell you that either?"

I shook my head. "I never asked. I didn't want to know."

"Well, now you know. At the end of the three months, he said he needed some closure, so he drove to Florence to see you. I told him not to go, told him it was a stupid idea, but he went anyway. A part of him had hoped that you would somehow convince your father to accept him, and when that didn't happen, he struggled to let go."

I hung on to every word. "Did he go?"

He nodded. "He stopped outside your gallery and saw you with your boyfriend." He didn't stare at me with accusation, but he didn't give me a friendly look either.

"Oh no…"

"He watched you two hold hands and look at your paintings. Then he drove off and came back here."

"No." I covered my face with both of my palms, humiliated that Bones had known about Antonio the entire time. He saw us together and probably made the wrong conclusions, that I was sleeping with someone else, that I was in love with someone else. I pulled my hands off my face and then stiffened. "Wait…he saw me with someone else, and he still helped my family?" I gave Max an incredulous look, unable to believe what I was hearing. "After everything my family did to him? After seeing me with someone else?"

He shrugged. "I said the same thing to him, but he didn't care. All he cared about was you."

I ran my hand through my hair as I stared at Max. I looked into his eyes without really seeing him, only feeling his expression stare back at me. Just when I felt a moment of happiness, it was taken away from me. Bones had always loved me, had loved me in a way no one else ever had. My father said he wanted me to be with a man who would love me more than he did…and Bones had always been that person. The time we spent apart never should have happened.

We always should have been together.

"I hate to be rude, Max, but could you leave?"

He smiled then winked. "I'm on it." He walked into the elevator then disappeared.

I headed down the hallway, my heart beating just as fast as the first time I saw Bones in that hospital room. I never doubted my love for him, and I knew he never doubted his love for me. Antonio was a man who was better suited for me, and Bones was the worst possible choice for a husband, but that didn't matter. I loved him with my whole heart, wanted to spend the rest of my life with him, and I would never let anyone break us apart ever again.

I stepped into his office and saw him stacking the last of his rifles inside the hard silver case. He was wearing a black t-shirt with black jeans, and his fair skin contrasted against the dark color, but his ink matched it too. He shut the lid and locked it before his eyes moved up to meet my expression. It seemed like he was going to say something, but when he saw the look on my face, he changed his mind. A rigid expression came over his features, and he watched me with intensity, waiting for me to make my move. He had no idea what I was thinking or what had triggered my deep reaction, but he knew it was something.

He lowered his hands to his sides and kept staring at me, waiting for me to make my move.

My eyes filled with moisture, impending tears that I never asked for. They coated my eyes and slightly blurred my vision. There was no reason to cry, not when I should only be happy. But Bones never failed to surprise me, to shock me to my very core. He was the first one to admit he loved me, and he'd said it without shame or hesitation. He didn't care about the stakes. He didn't care about the wrath of my family. He didn't care about the gun my father pointed in his face. Bones stood by me from the beginning, being the most loyal man I'd ever known. His past was irrelevant when he had become such a noble person. His father had caused a deep rift in my family, but Griffin changed his legacy by becoming a man who earned my father's respect—which was nearly impossible.

Bones grew tired of the silence. "Baby." He could issue wordless orders and ask me questions with just that phrase. When we communicated with our minds, words weren't necessary. Throughout our relationship, talking had never been one of our strongest points, not when we spoke to one another in other ways.

I came around his desk, watching him stare at me with his

formidable eyes. I moved into his body, pushed my hands underneath his shirt and up his hard stomach, and then rose onto my tiptoes to give him a soft kiss on the lips. When I felt his mouth, the tears came loose. They rolled down my cheeks and landed on my lips so we both could taste the salt.

He didn't circle his arms around my waist, and he kissed me with his eyes open, watching every reaction that I made.

I pulled back and looked at him, unable to think of the right words to express the way I felt. It was difficult to organize my thoughts when I could only think of my emotions. "Max told me everything." I rested my forehead against his chin, my eyes looking at his powerful chest. "He told me about your crash…"

He inhaled a deep breath, the annoyance heavy in the sound of his breathing.

"And he told me there was never anyone else…" My thumbs moved along the deep grooves of his stomach, feeling the riverbeds between the valleys. "I was too afraid to ask because I didn't want to hear the answer."

Bones said nothing, his arms still by his sides.

"I'm so sorry that I hurt you…" I was sorry he had seen me with Antonio, seeing something that wasn't really there. I was sorry my family had ripped us apart. I was sorry I didn't try to harder to keep us together. "And after everything…even when you thought I was with someone else…you still took that bullet for my father." I took a deep breath before I lifted my chin to meet his gaze.

He stared down at me, thick like a tree trunk and still like a statue. "You shouldn't be surprised, baby. Don't ever be surprised. I will guard you with my life. I will protect you as long as I live. I will chase away your nightmares every night. I'll keep you warm in the dead of winter. I will be the monster that everyone fears—but I will be your monster."

"You aren't a monster…you're a kind and wonderful man."

He wiped away another tear with the pad of his thumb. "Let that be our secret." His thumb moved to my bottom lip and swiped across it, rubbing the tear across my mouth.

"That night you saw me with Antonio—"

"I don't care about him. He was just a distraction, a boy to make you forget about a man. Even if you did sleep with him, it wouldn't make a difference to me. Because he is nothing compared to me. He is nothing to us. He never had a chance because he could never erase me. But I can erase him." He snapped his fingers. "Just like that. I'm the man you love, and I will be the only man that you ever love. Your body, soul, and heart all belong to me. I won the battle, and I conquered the Barsettis. It's not the revenge I wanted, but I got something so much better in the end—you. The daughter of my greatest enemy is now mine. Every broken bone, every drunken night, and every pain was worth it. It was all worth it to have you. So don't speak of the past ever again. Don't ever speak that boy's name to me again. Don't ever remind me how dark those three months were. All I want is the future—the quiet and simple future we've always talked about."

ELEVEN

Conway

The double doors to the terrace were open, illuminating the bedroom with natural light. Birds sang from the trees surrounding the house, chirping quietly as they enjoyed the summer sun. There was a gentle breeze, fragrant with the smell of grapes and olives. This place had always been peaceful to me, surrounded by hillsides and vineyards. My parents used to sit outside together on the back porch and drink wine while my sister and I worked on homework in the sitting room. There was something about the place that made feel comfortable, that brought me a strong sense of peace.

I didn't want to come here originally, not when I felt like a burden to everyone. But the truth was, I felt safe there. With my father watching the property and my uncle just down the road, it was the safest place Muse and I could be.

Since I was unable to take care of my wife, I didn't feel like such an asshole when my mother could help her with what she needed. I was on bed rest because of my broken ribs, which would take a few weeks to heal. I could move around, but it always gave me a jolt of pain. Going down the stairs was the worst. So I spent most of my time lying down or sitting. My injury didn't stop my wife from straddling my hips every night, so I still got the satisfaction I needed. Seeing her pregnant belly and swollen tits as she moved up and down was such an erotic sight.

I think I preferred her body when she was pregnant.

I was sitting up in bed with my laptop across my thighs while Muse sat in the chair beside me reading a book. She was in a white summer dress, a loose-fitting silk that gave her stomach ample room. Her hair was pulled back to reveal her pretty face, and every few minutes, she rubbed her hand across her large belly, feeling our child kick.

I set my laptop aside and stared at her, wondering if we were having a girl or a boy. The doctor knew, but we said we didn't want to know. When the baby arrived, we wanted to be surprised.

I preferred a boy over a girl, but not because having a son to carry my name was important to me. Having seen men gawk at women all my life, and after being a player myself, I didn't want my daughter to be the target of assholes like that. Having a beautiful sister was hard enough.

Having a daughter would be a million times harder.

When Muse noticed my stare, she looked at me. "Need anything?"

"No." Despite the peaceful landscape, I was growing restless with inactivity. My face started to look much better now that the swelling and bruising were nearly gone. It'd been two weeks since that horrific evening, and Muse was still having nightmares every night.

"You're staring at me, so it seems like you need something."

"Yes. I need to stare at you."

A soft smile moved over her lips before she turned back to her book.

With the Tuscan sun brightening the color of her dress and her hair, she looked like an image from one of Vanessa's paintings. "You're gorgeous, Muse."

A slight tint entered her cheeks before she looked at me, her eyes soft. "Thanks, Con…"

"I could look at you forever."

A knock sounded on our door. "Can we come in?" Mama's voice reached our ears.

"Of course." Muse set her book down and opened the bedroom door. "I was reading, and Conway was doing some work on his laptop."

Mama carried my lunch to the bed and set the tray down. "Lars made salmon in a bed of quinoa and a side salad along with an iced tea." She positioned the tray over my lap then placed the glass on the nightstand.

Every time my mother brought me anything, I felt worthless. I didn't like watching her wait on me, not when she'd done enough work raising me. I should be waiting on her hand and foot, not the other way around. "Thanks, Mama."

She examined my face like she did every day, just the way she used to when I was a sick boy with a fever. She placed her hand against my forehead to feel my temperature.

I wanted to push her hand off and tell her she was being ridiculous, but after everything she'd been through, seeing her only son in a hospital bed with a bruised face and broken ribs, I let her get her way. "I'm fine, Mama."

"Just checking." She ran her fingers through my hair, staring at me like I was I still a little boy. She hadn't looked at me that way in a long time. She usually treated me like a grown man, respecting me as an adult and not treating me like I was delicate. But the second I was hurt, she seemed to regress. "You look a lot better, but I still worry. Do you need anything else? It's almost time for another painkiller, but we can probably give it to you now."

"Really, I'm fine." I patted her arm.

Mama finally turned to Sapphire. "How about you, sweetheart? Do you need anything? Are you ready for lunch?"

"No thanks, Pearl," she said. "I've been having morning sickness today, and I just don't have an appetite."

"I understand," Mom said. "But you should eat something soon."

"I will." Muse rubbed her hand across her stomach.

Father came to me when my mother was out of the way. He sat at the edge of the bed, making the mattress dip slightly with his weight. He came out of the fight unscathed so he looked exactly the same as he used to, but the pain of my disfigurement was written in his eyes. "How are you doing, Con?"

"I'm fine," I said. "Just want to get out of this bed and move around."

"You'll get there," he said. "And if you don't, your mother and I have loved having you around. Stay as long as you like."

It was a comfortable place to stay, but I was eager to get back to reality. I missed fucking my wife as loud as I wanted. I missed taking care of her. I missed not having my mother bring me food. "Thanks, Father. You guys have been wonderful to both of us."

"Yes, it's been very relaxing," Muse said. "I've been so

worried about Conway, and it's nice to know I have someone to help me take care of him."

I didn't want my wife taking care of me either, not when she was nearly eight months pregnant. I wanted to wait on her around the clock, to get her ice cream in the middle of the night then rub her back so she could fall asleep. But my parents had been doing all the heavy lifting, driving her to doctor's appointments and making sure she took all her vitamins when she was supposed to.

Even if I wasn't completely back to full health when the baby arrived, I wouldn't care. I was going to be in that delivery room. I was going to hold my son or daughter. I was going to drive them home from the hospital. I refused to let anyone else do those things. "Have you heard from Vanessa? Is she in Florence yet?"

"No," Father said with sadness. "Haven't talked to her."

Mama cleared her throat. "She's busy. She'll call when she gets a chance."

My father was a constant worrier, and the mention of Vanessa made him fidgety. "Maybe I should call her. I just want to check in and make sure she's alright. It's been two weeks."

"Crow." Mama flashed him an irritated look. "No."

"I won't be on the phone with her long," Father said. "I just want to know—"

"No," she repeated. "The last thing she wants to do is talk to her parents right now. She needs space, Crow. Give her space."

"You don't think two weeks is space?" he asked incredulously. "How's Griffin's shoulder? Is he doing alright? Are they right down the road? Can I visit them? That's all I want to know. Two weeks is long enough."

Mama continued to glare at him.

I'd rarely seen my parents fight. I wouldn't really consider this a fight, but it seemed like it could easily turn into one.

"Look," Mama said. "I don't want to say this so bluntly, but your daughter has been reunited with the man she loves. She wants privacy, Crow. Catch my drift?"

Father immediately dropped his look, like he didn't want to acknowledge what she'd just said.

"She'll call when she's ready to talk to us," Mama continued. "And after everything that has happened, they deserve this time together. They aren't thinking about anyone but themselves right now—which is perfectly fine."

Father still didn't look at her, clearly uncomfortable by the subject. "What if I text her?"

Mama rolled her eyes. "Forget it, I give up." She turned to me next. "I'm glad you're like your father, but don't be too much like him."

I glanced at Muse then looked away. "I think it's too late for that."

TWELVE

Mia

My captor was an enigma.

The only thing I knew about him was his name—Carter Barsetti.

Sounded familiar, but I didn't know where I'd heard it before.

I hadn't seen him much for the past week. He left for a while to attend to business and had one of his maids watch me. I was chained up the entire time, even when I used the restroom. I didn't get to shower while he was gone. Like a caged animal, I sat there and waited for my owner to come home.

Owner.

I was a slave—again.

I lay my head on the pillow and looked at the ceiling, the skin around my ankle irritated because the metal from the cuff was suffocating. There was nothing for me to look forward to. I didn't have a TV or even a book to read. All I did was waste my life away by sitting alone in a bedroom.

But it was still preferable to Egor.

When I made my decision to go with the Skull Kings, I knew I was taking a serious gamble. But my master was so cruel, so psycho, that I had to assume a new master would be better.

But so far, I knew nothing about the man who bought me.

Other than the fact that he was young—and surprisingly handsome.

On my first day here, I saw him shirtless, in just his sweat-pants. He had tanned skin, Italian good looks, and his body was carved from marble. With dark hair and deep brown eyes, he was easy on the eyes. A chiseled jaw, furious eyes, and a nice mouth, he was the kind of guy you would hope hit on you at a bar.

Why did a man like him need to buy a woman?

So far, he seemed much preferable to Egor. For one, he hadn't hit me. I'd jumped out of his car and he'd caught me, but he never backhanded me. I came on a little aggressive, but he still didn't strike me. I called him a bitch-hole, but he never called me something derogatory in return. But then he pinned me to the floor and threatened to rape me.

So, he wasn't entirely good either.

But he was definitely a tremendous improvement over Egor.

If Egor ever tracked me down to retrieve me, which I doubted, I would have Carter to fight for me, since he'd spent a fortune on me. And while they fought like cats and dogs, I could run off.

But I didn't intend to wait that long. I would find an escape route before that—somehow.

I just had to learn about Carter, to find out as much information as possible about my opponent. Other than his name and the fact that he wasn't cruel like Egor, I knew very little about him. "Hey!" I yelled loudly, wanting to make sure he heard me from wherever he was. I hadn't explored the rest of the house, so I had no idea what it looked like. I wasn't even sure if I was on the second floor or the third. All I knew, based on looking out the window, was we were in the middle of nowhere—without a house in sight.

Footsteps grew louder, starting on the wooden staircase. He came closer, his footfalls sounding heavier with his approach. He wasn't a big man. On the slender side, he had narrow hips and ripped arms. His physique was comprised of prominent muscles and flawless skin. Just like before, he stepped into the bedroom shirtless.

I knew it was summertime, but the air conditioning was on full blast. "Do you ever wear a shirt?"

He crossed his arms over his chest and leaned against the doorway, his eyebrows raised in amusement, not annoyance. "Not when I have a woman tied to my bed." He cocked his head slightly, enjoying the subtle threat.

My heart pounded a little harder, but I did my best to hide it. "I've been chained up in this room for over two weeks now."

"And…?" He rubbed his hand along his jaw. It was free of hair, so it seemed like he'd just shaved. "Am I supposed to care about that?"

"I would hope so. You spent a lot of money on your new toy, but you don't take good care of it."

He pressed his lips tightly together as he tried to hide his smile. "You have shelter, a toilet, and food. During medieval times, these amenities would be considered luxurious."

Now it was my turn to cock an eyebrow. "Well, this isn't ancient times, and there's the Geneva Convention about prisoners of war. And this treatment isn't up to par with those regulations."

"You think those rules apply to me?" he asked with a laugh. "You aren't a prisoner of war. You're a hot commodity, a beautiful woman I bought for my own entertainment. I can leave you in here for a year if I want. I can let you starve to death. Doesn't matter—because I own you."

I would give anything to be able to break these chains and strangle this man. Egor reminded me that he owned me every single day, and now this man was repeating those disgusting words. I was tired of being owned, tired of being treated like second best. For every woman who'd ever felt powerless in this world, I had to do something about it. Instead of years of abuse breaking me down and making me give up, it invigorated a fight within me. I wasn't going to stop until I was free.

Because I had something to live for.

His smile slowly started to fade. "Pissed you off, didn't I?"

I brushed off the comment. "Take these chains off. You can't keep me like this forever."

"You bet I can."

"If you plan to keep me forever, this doesn't make any sense. And I saw the bandage you put on my ankle. What the hell did you put inside me?" If it was a birth control device, it was totally pointless. I didn't need one.

"A tracker."

"Then what do you need the chains for?"

"So you won't pull another stunt like you did in the car. And if you sit there and tell me you won't, you know I'll never believe you. I admire your fire, but I don't admire your stupidity. I underestimated you once, but I definitely won't underestimate you again. Now it's your turn not to underestimate me." He turned around and walked out of the room.

I didn't want to sit there for another two weeks with these chains around my ankles. I used to be locked in a hole in the pure darkness for days at a time. This was nowhere near that, but I still didn't like it. "Wait."

To my surprise, he actually turned around. "What?"

"If you don't underestimate me, then you should no problem letting me walk around the house."

He smiled again, in amusement. "The rest of the house is my turf. I have no interest in sharing it with you." This time, he shut the door when he walked out.

Damn.

SOME MIDDLE-AGED MAN I'd never seen before brought my meals to me. He seemed to speak only Italian, so I couldn't communicate with him at all. Days passed, and I wasn't giving the opportunity to shower. I was starting to get restless, needing to do something other than sit all day.

I was a prisoner, just like I'd always been, but this time, there was no threat of torture. Carter never came in to hurt me. He never came in to rape me either.

Not that I could blame him. I looked like hell from not showering.

But then, what did he want me for?

Why did he pay so much money for me to do nothing with me?

I couldn't figure it out.

"Carter!" I yelled for him at the top of my lungs, desperate to get his attention. Sometimes he came, and sometimes he didn't. I had no way to know if he was home or not.

A minute later, the bedroom door opened and he stepped inside. This time, he was dressed in jeans and a t-shirt, looking just as attractive with clothes on as he did when he was shirtless. "Yes?"

"Please let me go." I was never the kind of woman who

begged for anything, but I was starting to lose my mind. I grabbed the metal around my ankle. "It hurts so much that I can't sleep. I need to shower. Let me walk around the house. Let me watch TV. Do something…"

He didn't step into the room, choosing to hover by the doorway. "Is your request supposed to mean something to me? You're a slave, which means you don't have any rights. I don't care how uncomfortable you are. So just shut up and stop bothering me." He turned away to walk out.

"What the hell is going on here?" I snapped. "Why the hell did you buy me if you're just going to keep me in here? It's been two weeks. Men keep slaves for labor or for fucking. You haven't done either of those things. So, what is the deal?"

Carter stared me down with his cold gaze, giving nothing away.

"Tell me."

"You're in no position to make demands."

"I'm no position to do anything…so tell me. Why am I rotting away in here? If you can't trust me whatsoever, then I'm just a liability. And if I'm more work than pleasure, there is really no purpose in keeping me."

His eyes narrowed, full of hostility. "Would you rather I kill you?"

I didn't know anything about this guy. I didn't know if he would make good on that threat or not. A part of me, a big part, wanted to say yes. Being a prisoner for so many years had taken its toll on me. There were so many scars on my back that I looked like I'd been burned alive. I wanted this life to end, to close my eyes forever and never open them again. That wasn't a weakness, just admission of exhaustion. If my life never improved, then there was no purpose. But there was one thing that kept me going, one piece of hope that wouldn't allow me to ever give up. There was someone waiting for me, someone I could never abandon. "No."

"Alright, then." He turned away again.

"Carter, come on."

He stopped on the threshold then slowly turned around.

"Please. I'm not the kind of woman who begs…but here I am." I stood next to the bed with the chains around my legs. I brought my palms together and sighed, hoping this man would grant mercy on me.

Something I said must have changed his mind because he walked over to me and unlocked the chains around my ankles.

"Oh…god." I rolled my head back and rubbed my swollen ankles. "That's nice…"

Carter watched me, a new expression on his face.

I knew those moans came out inappropriately, but I didn't care. The shackles were too tight, and my skin burned from the irritation. It was nice to feel free, even for a short while.

He walked into the bathroom and turned on the hot water before he retrieved a towel. "Get in."

I walked into the bathroom then stood in the oversize shirt I'd been given. I waited for him to leave so I could shower. Whenever someone watched me in his stead, it was usually a woman, so I didn't care about changing in front of her.

He leaned against the wall, the steam starting to fill the room. "Take off your clothes, or don't shower at all."

Even though I'd been raped and beaten more times than I could count, I still hated taking off my clothes against my will. I still respected myself, still thought I should have the right to say no. So pulling those clothes off stung, stung just like it did the first time.

Carter looked at me, his eyes scanning over the old scars along my collarbone and forearms. My back was the worst part because Egor thought my front was too beautiful to defile. Carter looked at me with restrained sympathy, like he didn't want to feel bad for me but couldn't help it. But there was also a hint of arousal as his jeans tightened over his front, his large package forming a defined outline near his crotch. There was both darkness and light in him. He was neither good nor evil.

I'd been the recipient of a look like that many times, except Egor never showed me a hint of compassion. If I didn't sob during a beating, he wouldn't stop until the tears emerged. He got off to pain only, not pleasure.

I held my head high as I stepped into the shower and let the glass door close behind me. The warm water felt so good that I stopped caring about the man staring at me. My hair turned heavy from the water, but it also became lighter as the oil from my scalp was washed away. I rubbed the soap into my body and cleaned under my fingernails. Then I massaged the shampoo into my scalp and watched all the dirt and oil swirl down the drain.

The shower was so nice that I wanted to stay there forever.

When I looked out the glass, he was still watching me. As if there was a stunt I could pull, he kept his eyes glued to me. But after the few stunts I'd already pulled, he didn't trust me at all. He wasn't stupid. He knew I was a fighter, and I wouldn't give up until I was free.

So he would never stop watching me.

I shouldn't have underestimated him. I should have waited until the perfect opportunity arose before I made my move. Now, he would always anticipate it. But when he first bought me, I had no idea what kind of man he was. He could have been worse than Egor for all I knew.

Thankfully, he was much better.

I finished my shower and then dried off with the towel Carter handed to me. I dried my hair, moisturized my skin, and then prepared to put on the clothes I'd left on the bathroom floor.

"I have something else for you." Carter grabbed the outfit from the bedroom, a pair of jeans, a bra, and a t-shirt. "I think it's your size."

I took it with gratitude, finally holding real clothes in my hands. Egor never allowed me to wear clothes. "Thanks." I shouldn't have to express my gratefulness, not when I was the one with no rights, but I did anyway. I put them on and felt like a new person.

"Your ankles look pretty bad," he said as he stared down at my feet.

"Yeah...I've had solid metal wrapped around them for weeks. Gets old."

He walked toward the doorway and nodded for me to follow.

Was I finally getting to leave the bedroom?

"Let me give you a tour." He stepped into the hallway and then pointed toward the opposite end. "These are a few guest rooms, my office, and my bedroom." He headed to the spiral staircase and moved to the large sitting room that had several couches and a large flat-screen TV. "Living room. And here's the kitchen." He led me into a large room with a big kitchen island. There was plenty of counter space and a separate dining room.

"You live here alone?" It was a big place for one person.

"Yes." He opened the fridge and pulled out a few ingredients. "Hungry?"

I'd been eating nothing but sandwiches and chips all week. I was desperate for something more substantial. "Yes."

"Alright." He tossed a few veggies at me. "Wash these."

"You're going to let me help you make dinner?" I asked in surprise.

He got to work on the meat, slicing it into pieces. "I've got to put you to work, right?"

Just a few minutes ago, he'd made it sound like he would never allow me to leave that bedroom. Now, he'd abruptly changed his mind. It must have been the scars on my back that made him rethink his decision. He pitied me. I never wanted a man's pity, but right now, I would take it.

It made me realize that this man was more good than evil. He was aroused by my scars, but he also pitied them at the same time. Perhaps my standards for men had changed since becoming a prisoner because Carter's feeling and behaviors were still morally wrong.

But they were nothing compared to what I was used to.

"I'm going to cut you a deal." He sliced the meat on the cutting board before he set the knife down. He gripped the edge of the counter with both hands as he looked at me across the kitchen island. "Behave, and I will reward you."

"What does that mean?" I asked. "I don't speak dog."

He grinned at my smartass comment then laughed.

"What's so funny?"

"You remind me of someone." He scooped up the meat with his hands then placed it in a stainless-steel bowl.

"Who?"

"My sister." He moved to the sink and washed his hands with soap. Then he patted them dry with paper towels. "She's the sassiest woman I've ever met…until you."

"I like her already."

"I think she'd like you too." He snapped his fingers and pointed at the vegetables. "I told you to wash those."

There was another sink on my side of the counter, so I got to work. "You were saying…?"

"Don't try to run. Don't try to kill me. Don't be a pain in

the ass." He looked at me head on, his gaze turning serious. "And you could be very comfortable here. Don't give me a reason to hurt you, and I won't. Don't give me a reason to fuck you, and I won't."

What kind of reason was he talking about? He was the one who'd forced me to shower in front of him. "That sounds too good to be true."

"It's not. I don't want to chain you up in a bedroom any more than you want me to. I don't want to have to come to you every time you call out my name. I don't want the work that comes with managing a rambunctious prisoner."

"Then why did you buy me in the first place?" This man seemed to have everything. He was obviously rich, and he was obviously good-looking. He didn't need to buy a woman when he could pick one up on his own.

"Doesn't matter." He got to work on the sauce for the meat, pouring different spices and flavors into the bowl. "That can be our arrangement if you're willing to accept it. What do you think?"

I still didn't understand the offer, and without understanding what I was agreeing to, I didn't know what I was getting myself into. "I need to know why you bought me, Carter. Because, in my experience, men don't buy women to be nice to them. So what's the deal with you?"

He held my gaze, his temper starting to flare. "We aren't

friends. I don't owe you an explanation. I can do whatever I want with my money—no questions asked. Don't forget that you're still a commodity—and I still own that commodity."

I may have to settle for never knowing the truth. "What are your terms?"

"I already said them."

"Can I leave the house?"

He chuckled. "No. You can't leave the perimeter of the property—and I will know if you do."

"Okay."

He dropped what he was doing to look at me again. "If you cross me, I will hurt you. That's not an empty threat. It's a very potent one." He gripped the counter edge again. "I will have to punish you, to make you think those scars on your back were just a massage in comparison. Don't mistake my niceness for weakness. Do we have an understanding?"

The only reason I took his threat seriously was because I didn't know him at all. He was an enigma that made no sense. He bought me for a fortune but had no plans for me. He didn't outright hurt me, but he didn't respect me either. There was nothing more terrifying than being with someone with unknown intentions. When you didn't understand what a person wanted, they became unpredictable.

Carter was completely unpredictable.

If I the possibility arose, I might take it. But if I learned more about Carter, perhaps I could persuade him to let me go. He understood compassion, so it wasn't impossible. I would take the time to learn more about him before I made my decision.

I had plenty of time.

THIRTEEN

Carter

———————

I sat across from my prisoner at the dinner table. We shared a bottle of wine while we ate, and I had my phone out most of the time. I was exchanging emails with my assistant and going over my schedule for the upcoming week. After all the stuff that happened with Conway, my business had been put on hold.

She looked at me as she ate, and then she launched a smartass comment my way. "You're being awfully rude right now."

I looked up from the screen, my left eyebrow raised in shock. "What did we just talk about?"

"You told me to behave. And you defined good behavior as me not trying to kill you." She took a long drink of her wine, savoring it like it was the best thing that had ever touched her lips. "That's what I'm doing right now—not killing you." She took another bite of her food, eating quicker than me as if she was starving.

"I also told you not to be a pain in the ass."

"Well, you're being rude."

I locked the screen of my phone and set it down. "I can be rude all I want."

"And I can call you out for it." She grabbed the bottle from the table and refilled her glass.

Despite her annoyance, I was impressed by her quick wit. She couldn't fire off those comebacks without an impressive level of intelligence. That was the way my sister was. She was argumentative, but she was so clever that she usually won her arguments—even if she was wrong.

I placed my phone on the table. "There. You have my attention."

"I didn't ask for your attention. I just don't want you to bring your phone to the table. Even an eight-year-old knows better."

"Yes, but you aren't my mother."

"Good mothers raise good men. Maybe your mother didn't do her job well enough."

I could deal with her insults and her sassiness, but I drew the line when it came to my family—especially my mother.

"Don't talk about my mother like that ever again." My heart pounded harder in my chest because her insult bothered me all the way down to my core. I was livid, to say the least.

She must have understood that because she didn't rise to my words. She turned quiet, focusing on her dinner instead of me.

When she backed off, I picked up my fork again.

"This is really good. So much better than the sandwiches I was eating every day."

"Thanks." My sour mood still hadn't recovered. My family was the most important thing to me, and I couldn't handle anyone saying anything negative about them. I grew up watching my father defend his brother when he wasn't around, but the second they were alone together in a room, my father insulted him left and right. But only he could insult him—no one else.

"You're still angry."

I locked my gaze on hers. "Yes."

"Well, would it help if I apologized?"

"Is it possible for you to apologize?" I countered. "You don't seem like the type."

"You're right, I'm not. And I definitely don't apologize to men who kidnap me," she said coldly. "But I have a soft spot for mothers so…I'm sorry. I didn't mean to insult her."

"Thank you." I was close with my father because we had more in common, but I'd always been a momma's boy. My mom stayed home with us when we were growing up, so she took us with her to the store, made dinner for us, and spent all summer with us. She dedicated her whole life to raising us. She deserved all the respect she had earned.

"Are you close with her?"

"Very."

She was about to put a bite of food into her mouth, but she hesitated. It seemed like she was going to say something but decided against it.

"What?"

"Nothing."

"You were going to say something."

"Nothing you want to hear. Don't want to piss you off again."

I should just let it go, but now I was curious. "What?" I pressed.

She finished chewing before she spoke. "Well, if you love and respect your mother, it usually means you respect all women. I find it surprising that you think it's okay to buy a woman for your own amusement, considering your fondness for your mother."

She didn't know that I bought women with the intention of returning them to their families. In this instance, I looked like a bad guy. But since I couldn't tell her the truth, I had to pretend her opinion of me was correct. Egor told me not to tell her the truth, and I agreed with him. After seeing those scars on her back, I knew returning her to him was the last place she ever wanted to go. If I told her the truth, she would panic and become impossible to control. I still had two weeks with her. I didn't want to spend those two weeks keeping her chained to a wall. "She did her best to raise me right. It's not her fault I've turned into an asshole."

She dug her fork into her food and didn't continue the conversation. She didn't wear makeup because she didn't have any, but she still had undeniably beautiful features. Large eyes in the shape of almonds and thick lips that looked utterly kissable. She had long brown hair, and even when it wasn't styled, it was beautiful. It was the perfect length to wrap around my fist. She was a rare beauty, with natural looks that didn't require cosmetic enhancement. She was perfect all on her own.

No wonder Egor was willing to pay so much for her.

I'd been with a lot of beautiful women, models, dancers, strippers, all kinds. But I could honestly say I'd never met someone with her unique qualities. Her beauty stared me right in the face, but I couldn't put my thumb on the single quality that made her stand out. Maybe it wasn't her looks at all—but that smartass mouth of hers.

"So, what do you do for a living?"

A few hours ago, I'd released her from the shackles and watched her shower, treating her like an inmate in prison. Now we were talking casually, like two friends catching up. "Does it matter?"

"Just trying to make conversation." She rolled her eyes. "I can only assume your trade is in the criminal sector, so nothing you say is going to surprise me."

I didn't see the harm in telling her, not when she had no power over me. She couldn't run away, and once she was back with Egor, I would never see her again. "I own a car company. I design them and market them."

"You design cars?" she asked, genuinely impressed. "What kind of cars?"

I could talk about my work all day. Sometimes I got carried away and talked people's ears off. I'd done it on dates, but they didn't mind because success usually turned them on. "The kind you arrived in."

"Ooh…sports cars. That's cool."

Since I was so successful, people's compliments shouldn't matter to me. But flattery still worked.

"How do you design them? Do you design the look?"

"I design everything. I'm also an engineer. I have a team that helps me with other elements, like making cars electric or improving gas mileage, but I do the basics, from the interior to the exterior."

"Wow, that's impressive. I've never heard of anything like that before." She finished eating and set her fork on her empty plate. She'd wiped it clean, getting every single bite like she might not get the chance to eat again. "How long have you been doing that?"

"About ten years."

Her eyebrows furrowed. "How old are you?"

"That's blunt. How old are you?"

"Twenty-six," she said without offense. "The only reason why I ask is because you seem young to have had that kind of success for such a long time."

"I started young."

"Clearly. But that makes it more impressive. When I imagine a man saying something like that, I picture a guy in his forties—at least."

"I'm not in my forties." Not even in my thirties.

She pressed her lips tightly together as she considered her guess. "Thirty-three?"

"Twenty-nine."

She shook her head slightly. "That's unbelievable. You owned an entire car company when you were nineteen?"

"At that age, I was starting out. Had a little success. It slowly grew over the following year before it started to snowball. People like my designs and the power of my engines. Not only that, but people are impressed by my clean energy emissions. It exceeds the government recommendations by a factor of ten."

"Speak English, Carter," she teased. "Exceeds what?"

"The government regulations for gas emissions," I said. "Mine are the lowest in the industry without compromising on speed and power."

She nodded slowly. "Wow. If I had the money, I would buy one of your cars."

I chuckled. "Thanks."

She cleared the plates then carried them into the kitchen. I heard the faucet turn on a moment later, and the sound of her washing dishes and clearing the kitchen counter filled my ears.

I wouldn't let my guard down around her because she was still unpredictable, but it seemed like I'd neutralized her hostility. I didn't ask her any personal questions because I didn't want to know anything about her. If I sympathized with her, I might struggle to hand her off to that Russian demon. The second I saw those deep scars on her back, the evidence of severe punishment with a whip, I immediately felt sorry for her. A woman didn't deserve to be treated that way. But at the same time, I found it arousing. I'd never been turned on by pain before. I liked spanking a woman or grabbing her by the neck, but I'd never seriously wanted to hurt someone. But the idea of punishing her like that got me hard.

This woman did strange things to me.

SHE WATCHED TV in the living room with me, enjoyed another bottle of wine, and then I walked her to her bedroom.

"I feel like we're on a date," she said as she stepped inside her bedroom.

"That's a nice way to put it." I pulled the key out of my pocket and grabbed the door handle. "I'll see you in the morning."

She glanced at the metal key in my palm. "Are you going to lock me in here?"

"Yes. Need anything else before I go?"

Her eyes narrowed until they looked like two piercing bullets. "What about our deal? You said if I didn't pull anything, I could have a very comfortable life."

"I'm aware of what I said."

"Then you can't lock me in here."

"I can do whatever I want. I've given you a great deal, and you would be stupid to fuck it up. But that doesn't mean I trust you."

"What if I need something?"

I pulled the phone out of my pocket and handed it to her. "My cell number is programmed into the contacts."

She gripped it in her hand, staring at it like I'd just handed her a piece of solid gold.

"It's not a regular cell phone."

She looked up again, her confused expression becoming heavy with disappointment.

"It can only connect to my cell phone. So you can't call the police, a friend, or any other number."

She clutched it in her hand again before lowering it to her side.

"Good night."

She sighed before she turned away. "Good night, Carter."

Instead of shutting the door, I stared at her back, seeing the way she tossed the phone on the bed. "What's your name?" Egor never mentioned her by name, and at the Underground, she was simply referred to as a slave. In the weeks that I'd had her, it had never crossed my mind. I wanted to be as unattached as possible, so when I handed her over to Egor I wouldn't lose any sleep over it. But if I was going to keep conversing with her, it would be easier if I knew what to call her.

She slowly turned around, pulling her hair over one shoulder. The t-shirt she wore was loose on her curves, but the jeans hugged her tightly, showing her bubble ass and slender thighs. She looked at me with her light brown eyes, the color of young tree bark. "Mia."

FOURTEEN

Mia

Carter unlocked the door in the morning, letting me out of my cage like some kind of dog.

I told myself not to complain, not when I was able to sleep comfortably in the bed without a chain hooked to my ankle. I could shower when I felt like, pee when I felt like it, and I could look out the window all I wanted.

We were somewhere in between Milan and Verona, in the countryside, without another house in sight. He had olive trees around his property, and there was a high stone wall that surrounded it, keeping everything contained. He had a swimming pool, a nice terrace, and a spectacular garden. There was no way he took care of that himself.

He didn't wait around for me after he unlocked the door. He headed downstairs.

I followed him a moment later and examined my surroundings, finally exploring the house without him breathing over my shoulder. There was a picture mounted on the wall, so I stopped to look at it. Carter was in it, along with other people who looked similar to him. It seemed to be a family portrait at Christmastime. Of course, they were all beautiful just like him.

I glanced down the hallway and assumed the room with the partially open door was where he slept. His office was there too. I was tempted to sweep the place for stowed away guns, but he probably cleared everything—with the exception of his room.

I still hadn't decided what I was going to do about him. I could either try to kill him or convince him to let me go. He seemed to be a momma's boy, so that told me he had a heart under that hard chest. But the fact that he bought me at all told me he wasn't innately kind. If I laid my cards on the table too soon, he would never drop his guard and would know I would always be a flight risk.

So I had to do this carefully.

I walked downstairs and joined him in the kitchen. He had made a cup of coffee with the espresso machine.

"Can you cook?" He unbundled the newspaper from the rubber band and laid it out on the table. He pulled out the sections he wanted to read, sports, world news, and surprisingly, comics.

Cooking was one of my skills. I hadn't done it in years, but I used to cook almost every meal. "Yes."

He grabbed his coffee and headed to the dining table. "I want scrambled egg whites, a piece of toast, sliced tomatoes, and an assortment of fruit." He issued the command without even looking at me. He turned his back on me, the muscles under his skin shifting and moving as he carried himself. All the muscles of his back were precisely tuned, like he lifted various kinds of weights to work out each one. With tanned skin that complimented the dark hair at the nape of his neck, it was a nice sight. His sweatpants hung low on his hips, showing the muscles that flanked him on either side of his spine.

The sight distracted me for a moment. "That wasn't a very nice way to ask."

He didn't turn around as he stepped into the dining room, which was filled with natural light. "Because I didn't ask at all."

I reminded myself that making him breakfast was much better than the ways Egor expected me to serve him. He preferred to have large meals in front of me while I starved. Then he liked to beat me until tears emerged from my eyes. Only then would he fuck me, when he could listen to me cry.

This was definitely preferable.

But I refused to be grateful for it.

I whipped up the food he asked for and served it to him.

His newspaper was off to the side, and he was scrolling through his phone, checking emails. He didn't lift his gaze to look at me. "Thank you."

"Sure." Now that my job was done, I walked back into the kitchen.

"Sit with me and eat."

I came back to him. "Eat with you?"

"Yes." He kept typing a message. "You made something for yourself?"

"No. You didn't tell me I could eat." If I ever tried to eat without permission, Egor didn't refrain from strangling me, which was ironic considering he starved me in the first place. He pushed me until my breaking point then punished me for placing a piece of bread in my mouth.

He finally looked up from his phone, his right eyebrow arched. "You were waiting for permission?"

Maybe he thought it was a joke, but I certainly didn't. "Yes."

His incredulous look slowly evaporated, replaced by a look of sadness. He never asked me about my past, where I came from, and he'd waited a few weeks before he bothered to learn my name. He'd seemed indifferent to me.

"Well, you can eat whenever you want while you live here."

A sense of gratitude welled up inside me, and it was so strong that I nearly let tears form in my eyes. His gesture wasn't even that kind, but it meant the world to me. It was one of the few times I'd been treated as a human being in the presence of a man. He had more power than me, but he didn't abuse it like the others did. "Thanks." I walked back into the kitchen, made something for myself, and then joined him at the table again.

He read the newspaper, took a few phone calls, and then picked at his food slowly. He paid more attention to his coffee, savoring that more than the food. He didn't make eye contact with me once or attempt to make conversation with me. Then the phone rang again.

He nearly did a double take when he saw the name on the screen. He took the call quickly, hardly letting it ring. "Hey, man. How are you feeling?"

I couldn't hear the voice on the other line, but I knew it was someone special. Carter spoke to this person differently from all the others. He was excited, invested, and enthused. Even his tone was different.

"How's the wife?" He listened to the man talk on the other line. "I'm glad you're doing better. How much longer will you be staying with your parents?" He leaned back in his chair and looked out the window. "I've been meaning to stop by, but…I've had my hands full." His eyes finally moved to my face for the first time since I sat down. "Yeah, I'll talk to you then. Bye." He hung up and set the phone on the table.

"Who was that?"

"You're nosy." He picked up his mug and sipped his coffee.

"I only ask because he seemed important to you. You spoke to him differently from everyone else."

He set down his mug then looked at me, his brown eyes bright as they reflected the morning light coming through the window. His hair was messy because he hadn't showered yet, but the sleepy look suited him. I imagined the women he brought home loved that look every morning. So far, I hadn't seen him bring anyone home. If he wasn't fucking me, then he must be fucking someone. "My cousin. But he's more like a brother."

"Is he okay?"

"He had an incident a few weeks ago, but he's going to be alright." He didn't elaborate and didn't invite me to ask questions.

Now I knew he was close with his cousin as well as his mother, along with his sister. It seemed like he had a nice family he could always turn to. If he had people in his life, what did he need me for? "I've been trying to figure out why you want me around, but I haven't figured it out."

His hands came together in front of his chest. "Maybe you're overthinking it."

"I thought you'd want me for sex, but you don't look like the kind of man who struggles to land pussy."

The corner of his mouth rose in a smile. "Why do you say that?"

"Uh, it's obvious."

He narrowed his eyes on my face. "Not to me."

"Oh, come on. You're hot."

Now he grinned completely, the corners of his mouth rising toward the ceiling. "Hot, huh?"

Maybe Carter was a psychopath who was just trying fuck with me, to lure me into a false sense of safety before he struck. Knowing I could eat whenever I wanted and didn't have to wear a chain around my ankle made me feel like a real person. That gift of slight independence and freedom had improved my mood incredibly. But I would be stupid to assume it would always be this way. Men didn't buy women for a fortune just to keep them around. "A tad. So what does a man like you want with a woman like me?"

He shrugged. "That's my business."

"Since I'm one of the two of us, I think it's my business too. If you don't want to torture me or fuck me, then what do you want?"

His eyes darkened in a new way, locking on to my face with laser-sharp precision. "Who said I didn't want to fuck you?"

The air left the room with his comment, and the peaceful morning suddenly became potent with silent threat.

"I just said I wouldn't fuck you if you behaved. But the second you screw up your end of the bargain, I'll screw up mine." Without taking his gaze off me, he grabbed his coffee and took another drink.

I refused to break eye contact to show weakness, but I was definitely afraid of his words. I was afraid of the way they made me feel. It wasn't terrifying like it was with Egor. He never threatened me at all, just beat me and fucked me whenever he wanted. But Carter made the hair on the back of my neck stand on end with just his words. I felt the warmth in my belly, the mix of fear and excitement in my heart.

"And just so you know, I hope you do fuck up." He finally broke eye contact with me and picked up his newspaper again. "You can waste your time trying to understand me, but trust me, you never will."

"Why don't you just tell me? You bought me for a reason. I might fulfill that reason if it's not repulsive."

His eyes scanned back and forth as he read the newspaper. "Look, I bought you at the Underground to piss off someone." He tossed the newspaper aside. "He crossed me a few months ago, and I knew he wanted you, so I made sure I got you first. It was a pissing contest, is all."

"You bought me for fifty million for your ego?" I asked incredulously.

"Sweetheart, I'm a billionaire. I have so much money, I don't even know what to do with it. So just be grateful."

"Be grateful?" I cocked an eyebrow. "Why should I be grateful?"

He rested his elbows on the table and leaned toward me. "I don't need to know where you came from to understand what you lived through. The scars on your back spell it out for me. My company is preferable to your previous master. So, yes, be grateful."

A glimmer of hope erupted in my heart. "If you just bought me to piss someone off…will you let me go? Not tomorrow, but eventually?" I had to figure out how to escape one way or another. This man wasn't keeping me in this house. I had a life to get back to. I would either have to kill him or hope he would release me. He was the one who would dictate how that would happen.

He held my gaze for a long time, his eyes shifting back and forth slightly. When he was this focused, he looked even more beautiful. When he was angry, he seemed confident. When he was pissed, he seemed aggressive. With those muscles and good looks, he had the perfect package. "Never."

FIFTEEN

Bones

_____

After I visited the doctor and had my bandage removed, Vanessa and I left for Florence. I didn't prepare to put the apartment on the market just yet. She was anxious to see her family and get back to her gallery, and I wasn't in a hurry to get rid of the place anyway. It would just be more money in my pocket—and it wasn't like I needed that.

We took my truck, which was packed with all the essentials. I took a few rifles, shotguns, and pistols because I couldn't live anywhere without a stash hidden away. Even at the most peaceful times, danger was lurking behind every corner.

I didn't know if the issue with the Skull Kings had been resolved by the Barsettis yet, but something told me it hadn't been settled. The Skull Kings weren't exactly logical, and the Barsettis were too paranoid to make any moves of their own.

I wasn't sure what would happen.

I didn't mention any of this to Vanessa. She was happy right now—and I never wanted her to be unhappy.

Just like she did in my old truck, she sat in the middle right beside me. Her arm was hooked through mine while I kept one hand on the wheel. We used to drive around like this all the time, and sometimes she would sneak a few kisses against my neck. Her hand would glide over my thigh and to the definition of my jeans, teasing me.

I liked it when my baby was all over me.

I missed it.

I used to think about those memories every single time I was in my truck. That was probably why I crashed that night, the depression and the booze mixing together until it became combustive.

"Thank you for coming to Florence with me."

I kept my eyes out the window, looking at the open coun-tryside in front of us. There was nothing but vineyards, old cobblestone houses, and hillsides in front of us. It was a beautiful summer day—just like one of her paintings.

"I know it's not your first choice—"

"I want to be with you—wherever we are."

She rubbed my arm and then kissed my biceps, her soft lips brushing against my hard muscle. "I know you do." She rested her head against my shoulder and leaned into me, snuggling with me just like she did on the couch.

These simple moments were the ones I missed the most, when we didn't say anything to each other, but enjoyed one another's company all the same. Her affection was like a shot of my favorite whiskey. Sometimes it was even better than when she fucked me because touches like this were from the heart.

I never knew how much I needed love in my life until I had hers.

Her phone started to vibrate in her back pocket. It vibrated against the leather seats, so I could feel it too. She fished it out then looked at the screen.

Father.

Her family gave us peace and quiet for a few weeks, but I didn't let that fool me. I knew the second Vanessa and I were together again, I would have to see her family on a regular basis. Now that I was accepted among them, their presence didn't leave a bad taste in my mouth, but I couldn't shake the past either. Her father called me trash more times than I could count, and her uncle preferred to insult me with his fists. I knew it wouldn't be hostile when we were in the same room together, but it wouldn't be comfortable either.

At least Vanessa was mine. That was all that mattered.

She answered. "Hey, Father. How are you?" She answered with genuine perkiness, like she was happy to talk to her father.

His voice was audible on the other line. "Things are good. Conway is still recovering. His face looks a lot better, but the ribs are taking a little longer. He's restless, so naturally, he's moody."

"I can imagine," she said. "Never likes to sit in one place too long."

"No. Just like you."

She chuckled. "I'm better than him, at least."

"That's debatable," he said with amusement. "Anyway, just wanted to check on you. Haven't heard from you in a while…" The tension filled the silence over the line. Her parents had always given her space, but after what happened, her father was probably a little paranoid. "Wanted to make sure you're okay."

"I'm fine," she said quickly. "Griffin and I are halfway to Florence."

"Are you coming for a visit?"

"No. We'll be staying at my apartment above the gallery. Then we'll look for a house outside the city."

Her father paused for a long time. "You guys are going to move here?"

"Yeah."

He was quiet again, probably unable to express how happy that made him. "That's great news. Your mother will be thrilled when I tell her. Conway and Sapphire are going to start looking for a house once he's back on his feet."

"Wow, that's a lot of Barsettis in one place. Just gotta get Carter next."

"That would be nice, but Uncle Cane makes it sound like he likes it there in Milan."

"He'll probably change his mind when he settles down."

"Maybe," he said noncommittally. "So, how's Griffin?"

Vanessa smiled when she listened to her father ask about me. "He's doing well. The doctor just removed his bandage and cleared him. He's pretty much back to new."

"I'm glad to hear that." He wasn't as enthused as he was when he spoke of his own son, but he didn't sound bitter either. At the hospital, it seemed like he respected me because of what I'd done for his family, but that didn't necessarily mean he liked me—just tolerated me.

That was fine with me.

"After you get settled, you should come by for dinner," he said. "Your mother misses you… I miss you."

"I miss you too."

"I'm sorry for bothering you. Your mother told me not to call you…but I decided to ignore her."

"You aren't bothering me, Father," she said with a chuckle. "I'm excited to see all of you."

"Okay, good. Now your mother can't get mad at me."

"She'll probably be mad at you anyway."

"Yeah, you're probably right. I'll talk to you soon."

"Alright."

"Love you, *tesoro*."

Her smile fell. "Love you too, Father." She hung up and set the phone on the seat beside her.

Vanessa would be my baby for the rest of my life, so I knew I would have to put up with her family. When I heard her father wear his heart on his sleeve, I liked him a little more. He was the kind of man that was hard and tough, but he also loved openly. Only a truly fearless man opened his heart to someone—because he had something to lose. That was bravery. It would be hard for me to let go of the past, but I could move forward—for her.

At least he'd asked about me.

I kept my eyes on the road and didn't question her about the conversation. I knew she wanted to see her family, but I preferred hiding away and being alone in our apartment. I'd never been a fan of people, especially after I found Vanessa. As long as I had her, I didn't need anyone else.

"Conway is doing better. Let's stop by the house tomorrow to see them."

The only time I'd been inside that house was when I came face-to-face with her father for the first time. I handed him a shotgun, and he aimed it right at me. Handcuffed to the chair and vulnerable, I put myself out there in a way I never had before. But the bold step meant nothing to the Barsetti brothers. It would be strange to step inside that house again—under different circumstances.

She looked up at me. "Is that okay?"

Vanessa never gave me a choice in anything, just the same way I didn't give her one. I told her what we were going to do, and that was final. Perhaps Vanessa and I were so compatible because we were so alike. "Sure."

She studied my face for another moment, trying to look at my eyes through my sunglasses. "You don't like them, do you?" Her voice carried her melancholy, her heartbreak.

My discomfort around them didn't have anything to do with the blood war. I just resented them for the way they'd treated me for so long. Before I took a bullet for Crow, I'd proven my love for his daughter. I'd always been exactly what I advertised—a powerful man who could take care of her. Spending months being his punching bag didn't count for anything. What if the events hadn't unfolded the way they did? I would have lived the rest of my life without her. I simply got lucky.

"Griffin."

My arm moved around her shoulders, and I pulled her close to me. "A single apology can't erase the past, baby. Like I said, I risked my neck for you, not for them. I tolerate them, and they tolerate me. But no, I don't like them."

I CARRIED everything upstairs and into her apartment, and despite my protests, she helped me. She busted her ass up the stairs and carried things that weighed almost as much as she did. When most women would sit on the couch or do something else, she got her hands dirty. I didn't need her help, even with a bad shoulder, but her strength always impressed me. No matter what the odds were against her, she never shied away from a challenge. She was always eager to push herself, to be better.

She was strong.

Once everything was in the entryway, I took a look

around the apartment. It was exactly as I remembered it —and the painting of me was still on the wall in her living room. I'd wondered if she would take it down, but she never did.

She stood in the living room with her arms across her chest, releasing a painful sigh that reached every corner of the room.

I watched her, seeing the signs of sadness creep onto her features. She'd spent three months in this apartment alone, in the apartment I bought for her. My tenure of depression had nearly killed me. I was sure her time here hadn't been much better. "It's in the past now."

Her eyes focused on me, and after a moment, she gave a slight nod. "I don't know whether to be sad or happy. I'm sad because the last time I was here…I was miserable. But I'm happy that I'm not alone in this apartment anymore. I'm happy you're here with me." She moved into my body and rested her cheek against my sternum. Her arms circled my waist, and she stood there, clinging to me.

My hand slid through the hair on the back of her neck, and I stared down at the small woman in my arms. She might be petite, but she was strong and quick. The only kind of weakness she allowed herself to feel was at my expense. I was the only man she ever dropped her guard for, the only man to get close enough to actually hurt her. She felt the pain of heartbreak, wearing it on her sleeve the way her father wore his love for her. I never cared about the boys she took to bed before me. They may have had her then, but they'd never come close to her heart, not the way I had. Not only did I come close to it, touch it, but I conquered it. My possession of her was irrevocable.

She pulled her face away from the sanctuary of my chest to meet my gaze. "We should unpack…but I want to go to bed. I want you to make love to me." She ran her hands over my chest, her plump lips slightly open and ready for my kiss. The needy look in her eyes would be annoying on any other woman, but with her, it was the sign of ultimate commitment. She wasn't the smartass spitfire she was when we met. She allowed me to know her on a much deeper level.

I'd missed hearing those words from that pretty mouth. My hand tightened on her hair, and my fingers brushed across her bottom lip. We used to fuck exclusively, but then she wanted more, and I enjoyed it every single time I gave it to her. Now I lived for those words, lived for the tone of desperation in her voice as she said them. The only thing that could repair her broken heart was me, the passion, love, and desire I could give her.

My lips moved to her ear, and I kissed the shell. "I miss that."

She pressed her hands into my chest. "Listening to a woman ask you to take her to bed?"

"No." I pulled on her hair to make her head go back and so I could kiss her jawline as I made my way back to her mouth. "Listening to my baby ask me to make love to her." I lifted her into my arms and carried her down the hallway to the bedroom that had a queen-size bed. I dropped her on the covers then pulled my shirt over my head. My black ink covered all of my fair skin, the different images and words creating a work of art across my physique. My life was in the images and the words, the bloodlust and the heartache.

She held herself up on her arms and stared at me, watching me strip. Her eyes glazed over my body, the desire obvious in the way she parted her lips and took a deep breath. She pulled off her shirt next then unclasped her bra, letting it fall to the spot next to her.

I stared at her perfect tits like I hadn't seen them earlier that morning. They were firm and round, and I loved feeling them in my palms. They were small, but I loved their perkiness. Nicest tits I'd ever had in my mouth.

I dropped my jeans and boxers next, watching Vanessa's face turn vermillion with desire. She used to guard her expressions fiercely, to make her thoughts impossible to decipher. But once she fell in love with me, her emotions always danced on the surface. She wanted me like she'd never had me before. She undid her jeans and pushed them off along with her thong until she was naked on the bed. Then she opened her legs to me, begging me to join her in the sexiest way possible.

My cock twitched as I stared at her perfect little pussy. I loved this woman for her smart brain, beautiful heart, and the sassiness that oozed out of every pore. But as a man, I fell in love with the slice of heaven between her legs. It'd become the permanent residence of my cock, the dream house I'd always wanted. I wanted to stay buried there forever, to spend every lazy Sunday deep in her crevasse.

She scooted back to the headboard and breathed hard as she watched me. "Don't make me ask you again."

My knees dropped onto the mattress, and I made my way between her knees. I held myself on my knees, my hands touching her soft skin as I explored her calves and ankles. For the three months we'd been apart, no other man had come to this bed. No other man had been between her perfect legs. This was my territory, my home.

She looked up at me, her breaths deep and irregular.

"Ask me again." I looked into her deep green eyes, seeing the combustive desire that was about to explode. My hands squeezed the backs of her thighs, and my cock started to ooze from the tip. I made love to her the second I woke up that morning, not caring that she was still asleep. I was rude like that, taking my baby whenever I felt like it. But now I was desperate to have her again, like I'd never had her before.

Her hand pressed against my hard stomach, uneven because of the ripples of abs that were hard as steel. She moved to my hip then gave a gentle tug. "Make love to me."

"Please."

She was practically panting now. "Please…"

I grabbed both of her ankles and rested the bottom of her feet against my chest as I moved on top of her, my hands pressing into the mattress of either side of her small frame. She was petite and flexible, so folding her exactly how I wanted was simple. When she asked me to make love to her, she didn't just want me inside her. She wanted me to conquer her, to sink her into the mattress with my weight so she would always feel safe. She wanted to be my queen, to submit to her king. She wanted to be smothered by my love, to feel guarded and protected every single day for the rest of her life. When he was mine, she knew she never had to worry about anything.

I kept her knees together as I pushed inside her, gliding through that tight slit as her arousal smeared my entire shaft. I sank into her, getting her at the deepest angle possible, until my balls tapped against her ass.

She took a breath when she felt all of me, like she wasn't used to my size quite yet. Her nails dug into my wrists, and she looked into my gaze with a lidded expression. With parted lips and hard tits, she was ready for me.

I pressed my forehead against hers and started to move, to rock myself gently inside her and enjoy every slow second. I wanted to make this last, to make her come several times before I crossed the finish line. My job was to heal her heart the way she healed mine. Our separation had been brutal for both of us, stripping away all the joy that we cherished. When I lost her, I turned into a worse version of myself. She turned into a ghost. But now we would never know that pain again—because I was here to stay. I didn't give a damn who liked me or hated me. This woman was mine—and no one would ever take her away from me.

She dug her toes into my chest and sliced her fingernails into my skin, her breaths coming out deep and heavy. She pressed lightly against my chest to lift her hips so she could move with me, let me fill her over and over.

I rocked into her a little harder, making her tits shake with my thrusts. I loved watching her nipples harden, the color of her cheeks becoming deep red. The green color of her eyes became more vibrant when she was lost in the moment with me. She'd been that way before I left. She was that way still.

I'd never made love to a woman before her, but the second I had her, everything came naturally. My eyes locked on to hers, and I shared my soul with hers. I gave her everything I had, accepting everything she gave with greed.

"I'm gonna come…" Her hands snaked up my arms. "Already…"

I moved her ankles over my shoulders so I could smother her even more. Her feet rested on my shoulders on either side of my head. I folded her deep, manipulating her body like she was a doll instead of a person. "You're going to come more times than you can count."

"I expect nothing less…" Her fingers moved into my hair, and she stared into my eyes, her lips desperate for a kiss. She was too busy moaning to seal her lips against mine. She made love to me with her eyes as much as her body. She rocked with me and took my thrusts with vigor. Her spine shivered as she approached the climax that was impossible to ignore.

I was glad I hadn't been with anyone else in the last three months. They would have been disappointments compared to this woman. No matter how wild or enthused they were, they wouldn't have filled the hole in my chest.

They wouldn't have filled me the way she did.

I would have pretended they were my baby, would have pretended my life was still complete. But the second the fun was over, I would only feel worse about what I'd done —and missed Vanessa even more. "I love you." She was the only woman who ever heard me say those words. The first time I told her how I felt, I didn't hesitate. Confessing something like that didn't come easily, not for someone like me. But it was the simplest thing I'd ever done. There was no doubt how I felt about her. I didn't need to love another woman to understand what love was. She was my one and only.

Passion remained in her eyes, but emotion also jumped across the surface. She cupped my cheek and gripped my left hip. "I love you too." Before she even finished saying the words, her pussy clenched around me, and she was thrown into a powerful orgasm. "Forever...I love you forever."

I HADN'T SLEPT WELL in the last three months. It was impossible for me to fall asleep unless I was drunk, and unless I woke up still drunk, I remembered all the terrible dreams I had about Vanessa.

Having her back was an improvement for my health.

I was sleeping again.

I wasn't drinking nearly as much.

And I was happy.

But instead of sleeping all through the night, I would wake up at least once to look at her, to make sure she was really there. A part of me was afraid I would lose her again, even though that fear was unfounded. But if you'd ever truly been miserable, you were always afraid of being miserable again.

I'd already lived without her once. I couldn't repeat that.

She was asleep beside me, naked under the sheets that reached her shoulder. She was on her side and facing me, her lips slightly parted as she slept. Her face always looked the same when she was asleep, rested and beautiful. Some of her small teeth were visible. When she was awake, her fierce attitude made her a spitfire, but when she was asleep, she appeared harmless.

I watched her for a while because I couldn't go back to sleep. It was the first time I'd slept in a foreign place. The mattress was different, the atmosphere was changed. It didn't smell like her because she hadn't inhabited the place in so long.

I watched her for a few more minutes before I got out of bed and explored the rest of her apartment. I poured a glass of scotch since I hadn't had a drink all day, and I sat on one of the couches in the living room. The place was already furnished when I bought it, so these things had belonged to someone else. There was a small coffee table, a little TV, and a large painting on the wall.

It caught my attention because I knew Vanessa didn't paint it. It was an image of the countryside, of the endless vineyards, the Tuscan sun, and the summer heat of the valley. It reminded me of something she would paint, but the colors, lines, and angles weren't produced by her hand. It was definitely someone else.

I set my glass down and walked up to the painting. There was a signature scribbled in the corner.

Antonio Tassone.

A rock fell down my throat and landed in the pit of my stomach. It was like someone punched me in the gut with the butt of a rifle. It was a jolt of pain I hadn't been anticipating, a shock to the heart that made my fingertips go numb.

I'd never been jealous of him because I knew he couldn't compete with me. No man could. What Vanessa and I had was stronger than anything else she could have with another man. Even if she'd slept with him, it wouldn't have shattered my confidence. I would have made good on my word and erase him from her memory. But seeing this painting…gave me a rush of doubt.

They had a deeper connection than I realized.

He was an artist, just like she was. They obviously had a lot in common. She got this painting because it reminded her of where she grew up. Or he painted it for her because he knew it would mean something to her. Whatever the case, they had a deep relationship based on mutual interests, art, and spirituality.

For the first time in my life, I was jealous.

I hated this painting. I was tempted to take it off the wall and snap it in half. I wanted to douse it with my scotch then light it on fire on the sidewalk. I wanted to burn it until his artwork was nothing but ash.

I had to remind myself that she dumped him the second I was back. She made the call, which lasted less than five minutes, and it was over. There was no hesitation of where she wanted to be. Even if this guy was an artist she had a connection with, it didn't compare to what we had.

But I was still angry.

She didn't sleep with him. She didn't even kiss him.

I shouldn't give a damn.

But I did.

I finally turned away and returned to the couch where my scotch was waiting for me. I didn't want to look at that painting again. I couldn't stand the thought of looking at it every day while I stayed here with Vanessa. It would be petty of me to ask her to take it down. I didn't want to be that guy, to show any insecurity at all. But I also wouldn't tolerate her bringing it along to our new place in Tuscany. No way in hell would I allow that piece of garbage to hang on the wall.

My painting was still there where I left it, on the other wall. But I shouldn't have to share the space with anyone.

Light footsteps sounded against the hardwood floor.

Vanessa was approaching from down the hallway. I didn't make a sound, but she must have noticed I was gone when she reached for me in the middle of the night.

She appeared around the corner, her hair a mess from the way I'd fisted it earlier. Completely naked with beautiful olive skin, she was a living fantasy. Her dark hair, green eyes, and beautiful skin tone made her the most desirable woman on the planet. She squinted her eyes because she was still half asleep. "What are you doing?"

I was on the couch in just my black boxers. I held up my glass then took a drink. "Couldn't sleep."

She ran her fingers through her hair, her lids heavy with sleepiness. "Come back to bed." Her tone was potent with her bossiness. She turned around, expecting me to follow her.

Normally, I would. But this time, I didn't. I was pissed about the painting. Until that thing was off the wall and in the garbage, I would continue to be angry.

Her footsteps faltered when she realized I wasn't coming. She turned back around and looked at me. "Did you hear me?"

Despite my anger, I wanted to smile. I liked the offense in her voice, the way she got angry when she didn't get her way. She was used to having me whenever she wanted me. And when she didn't get what she wanted, her attitude fired up. "I'm not tired." I stared at my glass.

"Well, you can be not tired in bed. That way, I can get some sleep."

"You slept without me in that bed for three months just fine." I forced myself not to look at the painting on the wall, to give in to this strange feeling of insecurity. I assumed this guy was ordinary and forgettable. But perhaps my assumption had been wrong.

"What?" she blurted. "What's that supposed to mean?"

I drank from the glass.

As the anger pumped through her system, her eyes opened wider as she became more awake. "Did I miss something? What's going on?"

"I'm not tired," I said simply. "I'll come to bed when I'm ready."

She crossed her arms over her chest, her rage growing with every passing second. "I don't want to sleep another night without you beside me. I need to know you're there. The sheets get cold without you. I don't feel safe without you. So don't make me ask you again." She turned around and stormed off, her small feet stomping against the hardwood floor.

My anger hadn't abated, but I was even more amused. If that painting weren't on the wall at that moment, I would probably grin as my ego inflated. Nothing made me happier than watching my baby want me, watching her get angry when she didn't get enough of me.

I left my scotch behind and got into bed beside her.

The second my weight hit the mattress, she moved into my side and tucked her leg in between mine. She embraced me like a body pillow, her face resting against my shoulder while she hugged my waist. Like the previous conversation never happened, she went to sleep instantly.

I watched her sleep for a few minutes before my lips pressed against her forehead. That painting haunted me, but I had to remember the piece of artwork right beside me. She was mine to stare at forever. She was mine to treasure.

She was never his, not when she was always mine.

I WOKE up the next morning and did my daily one-armed push-ups and sit-ups. I usually hit the weights every day, but without my equipment, I had to exercise on my own. I made coffee afterward then sat on the couch.

I usually fucked Vanessa the second my eyes were open. I didn't give a damn if she was awake or not. My cock was rock-hard first thing in the morning, so I pushed myself between her legs and made us both come quickly before I started my day.

But today, I didn't do that.

The painting stayed on the wall, silently haunting me. In the morning light, the colors were more distinguishable. The brush strokes were visible. I didn't know shit about art until I started studying Vanessa's paintings. I could read her moods and emotions. When I looked at his work, I felt like I knew him in some way.

I didn't like that.

I needed to let this go. I was better than this. I shouldn't feel threatened by him, not when she dumped him.

But that painting constantly reminded me of him, played with my fear and imagination. I never asked about their relationship because I knew it didn't matter, but now I wondered about the specifics. That painting kept playing with my mind, turning me into a jealous psychopath.

I hated it.

Fucking hated it.

She woke up thirty minutes later, wearing one of my t-shirts that fit her like a poncho. Her feet struck the ground heavily as she stormed into the living room. With those angry green eyes burning into mine, she put her hands on her hips and exploded. "What the hell is wrong? We just got back together, and you're being an ass."

I stared at her blankly, surprised by her inaccurate state-ment. "How am I being an ass?"

"You disappeared last night, and then this morning, we didn't make love. We always do that."

"You mean, I fuck you when you're still asleep then leave?" I asked. "I didn't realize you found that so romantic."

Her eyes looked like two grenades about to explode. She stormed to me then smacked her hand across my shoulder. "See? You're being an ass. I know something is wrong. Tell me what it is."

I didn't react to her hit. She was small, but she could pack a serious punch. To me, the hit meant nothing. I rose to my feet and stepped away from her, unsure if I should come clean or not. If I kept it inside, I would keep pushing her away because it bothered me so much. The second that painting was gone, I could stop thinking about the man who tried to make my baby his baby.

Vanessa watched me, her arms crossing over her chest. Her eyes were still potent with rage. "Griffin."

I was too stubborn to admit the truth, to admit another man bothered me. But my rage was winning the battle, especially when the painting was on the wall right behind her. I could see both of them in my line of sight. I wondered if he'd given that painting to her as a gift, knowing she would love it after she told him about her childhood over coffee. Both of my hands tightened into fists.

She glanced at my movements before she looked me in the eye again. "I understand you better than anyone, but right now, I have absolutely no idea what's going on. Tell me." She stepped closer to me, dropping her hands to her sides.

I looked past her and focused on the painting. Artwork was supposed to stimulate the mind in beautiful ways, to bring a sense of peace to the home. But this painting tortured me, gave me heartache.

Her eyebrows rose in confusion, not understanding what my gesture meant.

I kept looking at it.

She finally peeked over her shoulder, paused as she looked at the painting, and then slowly turned back to me. She was still confused, but her eyes slowly started to fill with fear. She wasn't sure if I'd figured it out, probably because it seemed unlikely that I spotted his scribbled signature in the corner.

"I want that shit out of my apartment." My shoulders tensed as the rage vibrated through my body. Finally addressing the painting only made me angrier. Saying the words out loud only made me realize how much it really bothered me. Having it there was an insult. She hadn't had time to take it down because she didn't know she would see me in Milan, but that didn't sway my rage.

She was absolutely still, even her chest motionless because

she stopped breathing. All the anger she'd directed at me evaporated like it'd never been there at all. She didn't bother pretending the painting wasn't exactly what I thought it was. She didn't apologize for it either because she shouldn't have to. So she said nothing, knowing there was nothing to say to make this situation better.

"Now." I didn't want it to sit there for another moment. I didn't want it to infect the sanctuary of our home. I bought this apartment for her because I was her man. That asshole didn't deserve to have a claim on any of it. The only reason I didn't yank it down myself was because that would have made me seem petty.

She finally turned around and did what I said. She lifted the painting off the wall, the nail remaining behind. She turned it around before she leaned it against the wall, making sure it was no longer visible to the rest of the apartment.

That wasn't good enough for me. "I want it in the dumpster, Vanessa."

She turned around again, the sadness heavy in her eyes. "Let me get dressed, and I'll take care of it."

I stormed past her into the bedroom, pulled on a pair of jeans and a t-shirt, and then walked back into the living room. "I'm going out. That shit better be taken care of by the time I get back." I walked out without looking at her.

"Griffin—"

I slammed the door behind me, my arms shaking the second the closed door separated us. I stopped on the landing, gathering my bearings before I made my way down the stairs to the sidewalk. It was nine in the morning and I had nothing to do, so I'd walk around the city until my temper was finally subdued.

I knew I shouldn't be this angry, but logic was the loser in this fight. I'd suffered so much in the last three months. That piece of shit never would have given her that painting if I'd never been gone. They wouldn't have met in the first place. Now she was mine again, and I didn't want a single memory of that horrific period to be in my own damn house.

SIXTEEN

Vanessa
———————————

Once Bones told me what the problem was, it all made sense.

I hadn't even thought about the painting hanging up in the living room. I bought it from Antonio eight weeks ago, and since I hadn't been at the apartment alone since Bones and I got back together, I hadn't taken it down.

I never thought he would figure out Antonio painted it.

And if he did, I didn't think it would bother him this much.

He wasn't the jealous type, but he was definitely the possessive kind.

I didn't blame him for being upset. If something another woman made for him were in his apartment, I wouldn't like looking at it either.

I considered throwing the painting in the dumpster like he wanted, but that seemed wrong. Antonio had made such a beautiful painting, and it would be a disgrace to his talent to throw it away. Someone else could enjoy it. Someone else could love it as much as I did.

I carried the painting up the street toward his gallery. My heart pounded with the thought of coming face-to-face with him. Ending things over the phone was hard enough when I couldn't even see his expression. If I looked at him now, I would probably feel worse.

But he wasn't ever there, so I might get lucky and drop it off without interacting with him.

I stepped inside and spotted his assistant behind the counter. I actually smiled in relief, glad I wouldn't have to deal with him.

"Back again?" She smiled before she looked at the painting in my arms. "Oh no. Is there a problem?"

"No, no problem at all." I walked up to the counter and carefully set it down on the surface. "It's a beautiful painting, and I still love it. But I wanted to give it back...it just didn't work out."

"Well, we have a strict return policy here. We don't accept returns."

"I don't want my money back. I just want to give it back."

She examined the image for scratches and damage. "Just give it back?" she asked, completely confused by what I said. "I don't understand."

I didn't want to tell her my life story. It would be inappropriate since Antonio was her boss. "I'm moving, and I don't have room for it at my new place. I couldn't bear the idea of throwing it away, so I thought if I gave it back, you could find a better home for it."

The front door opened, and since I was the unluckiest woman on the planet, Antonio walked inside.

You've got to be kidding me.

He halted when he recognized me at the counter. Wearing a blue collared shirt with the sleeves rolled up and dark jeans, he looked exactly as I remembered. With a hard jawline, sprinkled fuzz along his mouth, and deep brown eyes, he was a handsome Italian who mirrored my own appearance. Looking at him reminded me that he was exactly what I wanted before I met Bones, exactly what I imagined in a husband.

But then I met the man I couldn't live without, even if he wasn't right for me.

The gallery turned quiet.

Tense.

A bit awkward.

He recovered from his surprise quickly and came to the counter. He spotted the painting and deduced what was transpiring. "Give us a moment."

His assistant grabbed her purse and walked out, probably taking her early morning break a little sooner than she'd planned. But she didn't challenge him about it.

Antonio looked down at the painting again, admiring his own work. "I'm hurt you don't want this anymore, but I suppose I understand." He picked up the painting and placed it in the back on a larger surface. His back was turned to me, so I couldn't see his expression. He took a moment to look at it before he came back to me. "But don't expect me to give you back the painting I bought from you." His eyes weren't kind the way they used to be. He was slightly hostile, like looking at me made me him angry. It'd been a little over a week since we last spoke, and that obviously wasn't enough time for him to come to terms with what happened. I didn't blame him. I took off without telling him what happened, and then I got back together with my ex without even telling him about it. After how patient and kind he was to me, I hadn't treated him right. If I weren't so happy with Bones, I would feel worse about it.

"I don't want you to give it back." My hands rested on the edge of the counter, my heart heavy from his sadness. I felt terrible that I'd hurt him, and I felt terrible for making

Bones jealous. I never suspected he would figure out the painting before I had a chance to get rid of it. He was too observant. "Antonio…I'm so sorry about everything. I really am."

He broke eye contact, looking out the window instead of at me.

I wasn't sure what I expected him to say. He shouldn't absolve me of my guilt, not when I was entirely at fault.

He turned his gaze back to me, but it was still full of the same melancholy.

"I was hoping I could give this back without running into you."

"I wish I didn't have to see you either."

Now I broke eye contact, feeling the sting of his words. "I don't want my money back. I just want someone else to have it, someone who will love it. This deserves to go up in someone's home. I couldn't throw it out…I just couldn't."

"Am I supposed to be flattered by that?" He rolled up his sleeves more.

This conversation wasn't going anywhere. The longer I stood there, the worse the situation became. Antonio didn't want to talk to me. He didn't even want to look at me. I should just leave him in peace. "I'm sorry that I bothered you…" I turned to the door, eager to get away from him. I hated the cold way he treated me, but I hated deserving it even more.

He sighed loudly from behind me. "Wait."

I stopped by the window and listened to his footsteps behind me. When I turned around, he was in front of me, rubbing the back of his neck with remorse in his eyes.

"I wasn't expecting to run into you…caught me off guard. I didn't mean to be such an ass."

"It's okay. I understand."

He slid his hands into his pockets and tilted his head slightly as he looked at me. "I guess I need more time to get over this. It was unexpected, and I was blindsided. The conversation was short and over the phone—"

"You have every right to be upset, Antonio. You don't need to explain anything to me."

He sighed again. "I've never wanted a woman so much. And then when I find one I really want…I can't have her."

His intense gaze made me uncomfortable, like listening to it was a betrayal to Bones. I lowered my gaze, unable to look him in the eye.

"I know I shouldn't say that, but it's true. I've always been honest with you."

Still unsure what to say, I said nothing.

He continued to stand there, like the conversation wasn't over. "Are you going to keep the gallery?"

I nodded.

"Are you going to keep living there too?"

"Not forever, but for the time being." I lifted my head, looking at him now that the awkward part of the conversation was over.

He clenched his jaw before he asked his next question. "Is he here with you?"

"Yes."

He gave a slight nod, accepting the answer, but only barely. "That's why you don't want the painting anymore…because of him."

"It makes him uncomfortable." That wasn't an accurate description of the way Bones felt. He'd flipped out, told me off, and then stormed out. I couldn't remember a time when Bones walked out on me. This was the first time, our first real fight. "And I understand why. He told me to throw it away…but I couldn't do that. I didn't want to. It's too beautiful of a piece…I'm not just saying that."

"I know," he said quietly. "And thank you."

Now that he was being civil, I remembered why I liked him in the first place. He was kind and easy to talk to.

"Do you still have feelings for me?" he asked, a hint of hope in his voice.

I didn't want to tell him the blunt truth, not when it would crush him. He shouldn't have asked the question at all. "It doesn't matter. He's the man I want to spend my life with. I was honest about that in the beginning, that he was the love of my life. The only reason I wasn't with him was because I couldn't be with him. But now I can. Please don't waste another moment hoping I'll change my mind. I can live without you...I can't live without him." I didn't want to hurt Antonio even more, but he needed a firm reason to move on. He needed a reason to forget about me, to dislike me.

He didn't react at all. His eyes remained on mine, unblinking. "He's a lucky man."

"Thank you..."

"Maybe we can be friends."

Bones would never allow that, not after the way he reacted to the painting. "I don't think that's a good idea. I'll always say hello when I see you. I'll never ignore you. I'll ask how your artwork is going...you can ask about mine. But no, I don't think we can be friends."

If he was hurt, he hid the expression deep down inside. "I guess that makes sense."

"You're a wonderful man, Antonio. You're handsome,

successful, interesting, and kind…you can have any woman you want. Someone just as special is out there. When you find her, you'll forget about me. When you find someone you love the way I love Griffin…you won't even remember my name. And that's a promise."

BONES DIDN'T COME BACK to the apartment until the late afternoon.

I unpacked all our things and cleaned up the place. Antonio had never come inside my apartment, so I didn't have to hide any other trace of him. I was eager for Bones to come home, but I was also dreading it at the same time. Knowing him, he would be just as furious as when he left.

I covered the nail on the wall with a new painting, one I'd painted after he left that no one had bought. It was an image of him in my bed, the sheets around his waist. His face wasn't visible, but his hard body and tattoos were detailed. I didn't remember every single tattoo he had, but I'd remembered a lot of them. Maybe when he saw that, he would remember that Antonio didn't matter… that he never compared.

He finally walked inside after three in the afternoon, and like I expected, he looked just as pissed as when he left. He wore a permanent scowl of displeasure, his eyebrows furrowed and his eyes two balls of burning fire. All the individual muscles in his arms were tight because he was flexing his entire body at one time.

His gaze landed on me first, still potently hostile. It seemed like he'd walked out five minutes ago, not five hours ago. He must have walked around Florence with that expression, terrifying everyone he passed on the sidewalk. People probably crossed to the other side of the road just to avoid him.

He turned his head toward the wall, to make sure the painting was gone like he ordered. He stopped for a moment to stare at the replacement, to see the painting I created from memory. He paused to look at it, to see the details I'd memorized after he was gone. He must have recognized his tattoos, the exact replica of his strong body. I didn't need his picture to recreate his image. Like the back of my hand, I knew every single detail, every dot of ink, every scar.

He turned back to me, less angry but still hostile.

I knew this fight wasn't over. It was only beginning. I stood up with my arms across my chest, the couch between us.

He stood rigidly, his arms still tensed by his sides. His muscular shoulders stretched the cotton of his t-shirt. Even when he was covered in his clothing, the strength of his body couldn't be denied. He stretched everything, from his jeans to the back of his shirt. He showed the same look he used to give me when we met, a look that suggested he hated me and wanted me at the same time.

I waited for him to say something, to figure out exactly what his mood was. But of course, he could handle endless silence since there was no level of intensity that made him uncomfortable. He could hold this intimacy for hours, refusing to say anything until I spoke first.

"I didn't have a chance to take it down," I said. "And I wasn't thinking about him or his painting, so the thought didn't even cross my mind. It's gone now, so let's move on."

His eyes narrowed slightly, his eyebrows furrowing at the same time. The second he cocked his head slightly, I knew he didn't like what I'd said. "Let's move on? Are you fucking kidding me?" He pronounced every syllable coldly, as if he was disgusted by what I'd just said.

I'd never seen him so jealous before. He was always so confident about himself, but one painting drove him mad. "You didn't care about him before. I tried to explain the relationship to you, and you said you didn't care. You didn't even ask if I slept with him. It's just a painting, Griffin. What is the big deal?" I never kissed Antonio, hardly touched him. Bones had no reason to feel threatened by him.

"What's the big deal?" His voice turned quiet, making it

far more menacing. He walked toward me slowly, circling around the couch like a predator about to pounce on his prey. His eyes stayed on me, his threatening arms by his sides. "It's a huge fucking deal. He's a painter, Vanessa. A damn painter."

"What does that matter?"

He stopped ten feet away from me, his gaze becoming even more terrifying. "If you fucked the guy because you were depressed and lonely, it wouldn't have mattered to me. That doesn't mean he ever meant anything to you. For all my life, sex has been meaningless. I don't even remember the women who have been in my bed. I don't remember their faces because the only face I care about is yours. But this guy makes art that reminds you of your childhood to put on your wall. The two of you have a connection. He doesn't just paint, he's good at it. I knew it wasn't one of your pieces the second I looked at it. It's not your brushwork and it's not your color scheme, but it also reminded me of you the second I saw it."

I listened to everything he said, following his train of thought with surprise. Since Bones didn't ask anything about Antonio, I never told him about the relationship. I didn't mention how we met or what our relationship was like. It didn't seem important to him. But now that he knew Antonio was also an artist, he was threatened. I never told him about the connection the two of us had. That's what made him angry, that I'd connected with another man even if I'd never slept with him. It was more emotional and intimate than sex ever could be. I could see the way it ate him from the inside out.

He stepped closer to me but kept several feet in between us. "Did he paint that for you?"

I didn't want to answer this question. I didn't want to talk about this anymore. "Griffin, I picked you. I only want you. Let's forget about him and be happy."

As if he didn't hear my answer, he repeated his question. "Did he paint that for you?"

I tightened my arms over my chest. "I told him I was still in love with you and I wasn't ready for a relationship. So we just spent time together as friends. There was nothing else there, Griffin."

He took another step closer to me, his eyes hardening. "Don't make me ask again."

The last thing I wanted to do was tell him the truth. I didn't want to hurt him, and I didn't want to think about the past when it had nothing to do with our future. "No, he didn't paint it for me."

His right eyebrow rose, and instead of being satisfied with that answer, he pressed for more. "Then why was it in your apartment?"

"Griffin—"

"I have the right to know."

"Forget about him. I have."

He ignored those words. "Vanessa."

"Why does it matter?" I demanded. "Whether he meant anything to me or not, you mean more. You're the man I love. I never loved him. Let this go."

He clenched his jaw tightly, as if he was struggling with his own emotions. His eyes shifted back and forth as he looked into mine, deciding how he would proceed next. He knew he should drop this, that getting worked up over some guy didn't matter. But looking at that painting ignited his insanity. "It matters to me."

"I never asked about what you did in the three months we were apart—"

"I jerked off and slept alone. Every night. End of story."

"And I did the same thing. End of story."

"No," he snapped. "You were going on dates, talking about artwork, sharing your passion."

This was a nightmare that would never end. "I never went on a date with him. When he asked me out, I told him I wasn't ready."

"Tell me how that painting got there."

He was never going to let this go, was he? "Fine." I threw

my arms down. "He came by my gallery as a customer. Took a look around and bought one of my paintings. Then he left. I had no idea who he was or that he was a painter himself. Then about a week later, I was out with Carmen when I noticed a painting in the window. I loved it, so I walked inside and bought it. Later, I learned that he was the artist. When he realized we bought each other's paintings without realizing it, he asked me out. I said no. That's the story, Griffin."

As he soaked in the story word for word, his appearance began to change. No longer angry, his entire body began to soften, but not in relief. Anguish moved into his eyes, and he wore an expression similar to the one he wore the day he left me. His breathing picked up, and his nostrils flared slightly. It was the first time he broke eye contact with me, like looking at me only caused him pain. He stepped back, his eyes shifting back and forth as he processed what I'd said. "You bought each other's paintings…"

"It doesn't matter, Griffin. The second you were back in my life, I forgot he existed."

He didn't listen to a word I said. He ran his hand through his short hair and down the back of his scalp. Over-whelmed with misery, he didn't know what to say. His spine wasn't straight anymore, and his shoulders weren't rounded. His posture turned weak.

"Griffin…"

He turned to the door, dismissing the conversation.

"Griffin." I followed him to the entryway. "Do not walk out on me——"

He walked out the front door and slammed it in my face.

He left me——again.

SEVENTEEN

Bones

I drove my truck out of Florence and into the heart of Tuscany.

There was only one person I wanted to see right now.

Vanessa's answer was even worse than what I imagined. They bought each other's paintings without even realizing it. I wasn't a romantic guy, but I knew that meant something. Stuff like that didn't just happen.

They had a deep connection.

She loved only me, and that's all that should matter.

But it bothered me.

Infuriated me.

Because none of that would have happened if her father hadn't stuck his nose where it didn't belong. None of that would have happened if I'd been given the chance I deserved. During those three months, Vanessa met a man who easily could have become her husband. Based on the small amount of information I knew about him, he sounded like her other half. What were the odds that the two of them would find each other that way? By falling in love with each other's artwork?

Of course he went after her.

He went after my woman.

I gripped the steering wheel until my knuckles turned white, and I was tempted to punch out the side window just to feel something shatter against my hand. The victim of my beating should be Antonio, but that wouldn't be right.

Only one person deserved the beating of a lifetime.

Thirty minutes later, I pulled up the house I'd only entered once. It was a place I'd never felt welcome, not even now. I killed the engine, stormed up to the door, and then banged my fist hard against the wood.

Then I waited.

My temple was pounding as the adrenaline circulated in my veins. All the muscles in my arms were tense, ready for the fight that was about to happen. This man had taken everything away from me.

I despised him.

A minute later, Mrs. Barsetti opened the door. "Griffin?" She spoke with surprise, but there was a smile on her face. It was the first time I'd ever seen her smile at me. It was the first time she'd looked pleased to see my face, despite how angry I must have looked. "I didn't know you guys were stopping by."

"I want to see Crow." I could barely get the words past my clenched jaw. I could barely keep my hands still because I wanted to yank the door off the hinges.

She picked up on my intensity. "Uh, is everything alright? Is Vanessa with you?"

"I want to see Crow." I turned my back on her and stepped away from the house until my feet hit the gravel of the driveway. I didn't hate her as much as Crow, but right now, I didn't like her either.

She didn't ask me any more questions and disappeared.

It seemed like a lifetime later before Crow finally showed his face. He shut the door behind him then approached me, his boots hitting the concrete before they crushed against the gravel. "Griffin."

I surveyed the landscape of the vineyards for another second before I turned around and faced him. He stood in front of his three-story mansion, a man full of so much wealth he didn't have enough places to stash his money. Not only was he wealthy, but that privileged life had been handed down to his children as well. A man with a perfect life, he thought he was a god who could do whatever he wanted.

I looked at him, my blood boiling when I saw his stern expression. With dark hair like Vanessa and the same olive skin, he was clearly her father. He showed the signs of strength despite his age, and after seeing him in battle, I knew he was a man worth his salt. Fearless, strong, and selfless, he would give his life for his son in a heartbeat—I saw it with my own eyes.

He watched me, his shoulders tense as he studied me with trepidation. "What is it?"

"I had to walk into her apartment, the apartment I bought for her, and see that goddamn painting on the wall."

He kept his expression blank, maintaining a poker face even though he must have been confused.

"She bought his painting, he bought hers, and that's where it all began—like a goddamn fairy tale. I don't need to hear any more of the story to understand how it goes, to know that Vanessa found a perfect man whom she connected with." I shook my head, doing the best I could not to punch him in the face. "Of course, you approved of him. A successful painter with his own gallery. A nice young man from a good family. I'm sure you dug into him and couldn't find a single flaw. Then you encouraged your daughter to date him, to forget about the psychopath criminal that she loves. You got what you wanted—for her to forget about me."

As the conversation continued, he slowly narrowed his eyes and he erected his walls, knowing this conversation would only get worse.

"I worked my ass off to get your approval." I pointed my finger in his face since he was slightly shorter than me. In his black t-shirt and jeans, he had a corded neck and a hard jawline. He might not be afraid of me, but he was thirty years older than me and not nearly my size. I could crush him—and we both knew it. "I gave you free labor, put up with your brother's bullshit, and listened to you call me trash. Fucking trash. Do you think that painter boy would have put up with that?" I slammed my fists into my chest. "Do you think that painter boy could have handled that? Do you think any other man in the world would have done that for your daughter? But did that mean shit to you? No. That asshole didn't have to do a damn thing for you to like him. But me…I was never given a chance. You stuck your nose where it didn't belong, and you took away the one thing that meant something to me." I slammed my hand into my chest again. "I've got nothing but my self-made fortune and my boys. I don't have a family. She was everything to me. I worked my ass off for her, but you wouldn't let me have her. So some other asshole got his shot. He fell for my woman. She never loved him, never slept with him, but that doesn't matter. In time, it would have happened. In time, she would have loved him. And that's all because of *you*." I pointed my finger in his face, not having an ounce of respect for him. "You know what my life was like for those three months? All I did was work and drink. Too depressed to go on, I drank until I lost my mind. I crashed my truck and ended up in a hospital. I spent all my nights alone, trying not to think about the one person I wanted to be with. And that's all because of *you*."

His features softened slightly, but he remained as stern as ever.

"I didn't save you and your son because I gave a damn about you. I couldn't care less whether you lived or died. She was the only thing I cared about. If she lost you, she would have been more devastated than when she lost me. That's the only reason I took that bullet for you. I was taking it for her because she would have died if you died. Make no fucking mistake, Crow Barsetti, I don't like you. I will never like you. I will tolerate you because of Vanessa. I will shake your hand because it makes her happy. I will treat your wife with respect because she's the mother of the woman I love." I stepped closer to him, getting right in his face. "But I hate you the way you hated me. Now it's your turn to earn my respect, my approval. But don't waste your time—because I'll give you the same chance you gave me." I stepped back, knowing I had to move. Otherwise, I might actually throw a punch. "Fuck. You."

Crow took all my words with the same stern expression, his eyes locked on to mine without blinking. He didn't show anger or hurt. He showed nothing at all, internalizing what I said in silence.

I finished what I came to say, dumped all of the blame on the person who should take all the credit. If Conway hadn't pissed off the Skull Kings and got himself in harm's way, I wouldn't be with Vanessa right now. She would have ended up with Antonio, and I probably would have put a gun in my mouth and pulled the trigger. This man had far too much control over my life, and I was done with it.

Finished.

EIGHTEEN

Vanessa

Bones didn't come home until later that night.

My calls didn't go through because he'd turned off his phone.

This wasn't how I wanted our relationship to be. We just got back together, and now we were fighting. Things had never been this tense between us, even when we were at our lowest point. That painting had ripped us apart.

He walked in the door shortly after eight.

"Thank god you're home." I jumped up from the couch, still in his t-shirt because I didn't leave the house all day. I didn't leave because I didn't want to miss him if he came home.

He barged inside with the same anger as before. It was like the last five hours hadn't happened. He was constantly livid, storming in and out of the apartment like a soldier marching into battle.

"You're still angry?"

He walked up to me, the same venom in his eyes as before. "You tell me."

I did my best not to roll my eyes because I knew that would just make the situation worse. "Griffin, let it go."

"I'll let it go when I feel like it. And I don't feel like it right now."

"We just got back together. I don't want to fight—"

"We shouldn't have broken up in the first place. Your father is a fucking piece of shit who needs to mind his own damn business. And if I hadn't taken that bullet, you might be marrying this guy."

There were so many things wrong with what he said, and the comment about my father rubbed me the wrong way. He might have the right to say it, but I didn't want to listen to it. "I know you're angry, but please don't talk about my father that way. I'll let that one slide...this time."

He clenched his jaw. "How generous."

"And who knows if I would have married him. It doesn't matter because it didn't happen."

He shook his head. "But it would have happened. This

guy isn't just some random guy. He sounds perfect for you."

"You don't know him!"

"Then tell me I'm wrong." The vein in his forehead throbbed. "Tell me."

I crossed my arms over my chest and sighed. "I'll tell you this. If I had married Antonio somewhere down the road, and hypothetically, my father changed his mind about you, I would have left him in a heartbeat. Even if I had kids, I still would have left him. At any point in time, even if I was old, I still would have left him for you. Maybe Antonio is perfect for me. But it doesn't matter how perfect he is because I only want you." I placed my hand on his chest, right over his heart. "He asked me out, and I said no. I told him I wasn't ready, so he said he would wait until I was. We had coffee a few times, hung out at the gallery a few times, held hands once or twice. I was attracted to him and knew I would want to be with him once I was ready. That's the full story. But then you were back in my life…and the last six weeks didn't matter. He didn't matter." I moved closer to his chest and rested my forehead against his sternum. My hands held on to his hips so he wouldn't slip away from me. "You're the man I want to make love to every night. You're the man I want to marry. You're the man I want to have kids with. You're the man I want to be buried next to for all eternity. You." I grabbed his arms and squeezed them. "Just you."

He continued to breathe hard, but he didn't move from my grasp. After a few minutes, he rested his chin on my head then circled his arms around my waist. He pulled me tighter against him, his powerful body coiling around me like a snake. His hand cupped the back of my head, and finally, the fight was over.

"You never have to be threatened by anyone, Griffin. You're the love of my life." I pulled my face away from his chest so I could look up into his eyes, to search for the softness I hoped I would find.

He wasn't angry anymore, but he wasn't himself either. "I'm not threatened by the boys before me. I'm not threatened by the boys who look at you and fantasize about you. I'm not threatened by a boy you might have liked." His hand moved through my hair, keeping it from my face so he could look at all my features. "But I am scared of a man who can make something that beautiful, of a man who can make my woman feel something. I'm scared of a man who can connect with my woman in a way I can't. I'm not ashamed to admit that terrifies me… because I'm not afraid to wear my love on my sleeve. When it comes to you, my heart is on the outside of my body. I keep it in the open because I want to love you so deeply, but that also means it's much easier to scar." Both of his palms cupped my cheeks.

"You do connect with me in the same way. You've always believed in my artwork. You've always appreciated it. I wouldn't have my own gallery if it weren't for you. I wouldn't have dropped out of school if it weren't for you. I wouldn't have reached this kind of success without my man believing in me. So don't think for a second that you don't understand me the way he does, that we don't have that same special emotional spectrum. Ours is deeper, Griffin. So much deeper. You don't need to make a painting for me to feel you." My hand moved to his heart. "Because I always feel you…deep inside me…every day."

He took a deep breath, this time in obvious relief. The monster had finally been calmed, and he retracted his teeth and claws. He kissed my forehead before he placed his head against mine. He continued to cup my cheeks as he held me there, his eyes closed. "Baby?"

"Yes?" I gripped his wrists.

"Make love to me."

The smile spread across my lips, recognizing the words I said to him on a constant basis. I was needy when it came to him, telling him exactly what I wanted and how I wanted it. He always delivered, more than happy to fulfill my demands. Now I wanted to do the same for him, to give him whatever he asked for.

My arms circled his neck, and I kissed him, feeling the softness of his lips and the coarseness of his facial hair. I breathed into his mouth as I scooted him back toward the couch, ready to ride him nice and slow. When the backs of his knees hit the couch, I pushed him back and straddled his hips.

He sat back and stared at me, slight arrogance in his eyes. He undid his jeans and pushed them down with his boxers until his cock was free. He yanked on my panties and stretched them to the side, not bothering to take them off because that would take longer than he was willing to wait.

I pulled the shirt over my head and then settled on top of him, my hands gripping his shoulders.

He gripped my ass cheeks and lifted me slightly so he could direct his dick inside me. Then he pulled down on my hips and pushed himself up, making his cock sink all the way inside me.

I lowered myself until I had him completely inside me, every single inch. We'd been fighting all day, but that didn't stop me from growing wet the second the fight was over. My pussy was always ready for him, ready for him to fill me. There had been no morning sex that day, so my body had been waiting for it all day. My hands pressed against his chest, and I breathed into his mouth. He was finally inside me where he belonged, long and thick. I watched the arousal in his eyes, the possession he always showed when his big dick was inside me. I moaned before I even started to move.

He squeezed my ass cheeks while his eyes remained

locked on mine. Full of power, strength, and surging arousal, he was thinking about the fight we'd just had. All he was thinking about was me, the woman who was sitting in his lap. Antonio was finally an afterthought, and it was just the two of us.

Boned pressed a kiss to my collarbone then trailed kisses all the way up to my ear. "Nice and slow, baby. That's how I want it." His large hands gripped my waistline and then guided me up and down, directing my pace down his shaft. His large shoulders rested against the couch, and he pressed his big feet to the ground to raise his hips to meet my movements.

His chest was twice my width and three times my size. I could easily rest both of my arms against him, from my elbow to my fingertips. I leaned against him for support, my hips rolling dramatically to push him inside me. "Stop." He was pushing up against me, making an effort when he should be sitting still. "My turn." When I asked him to make love to me, I lay there while he did all the work. He fulfilled my fantasies, making me feel like the most desirable woman he'd ever been with. He made me feel loved, like I was the only woman who'd ever graced his sheets.

He stopped raising his hips and sank deeper into the couch. He was a man who liked to always be in control, to do all the fucking when we were together. But he enjoyed it when I took the reins and gave a good performance. His jaw tightened as he felt me push my tight pussy down onto his length over and over. I was wet, and every time he was fully inside me, he winced like the pleasure was too much.

I pressed my palms into his hard pectorals. "I love you."

He gripped my waist tighter, squeezing me while an animalistic growl came from his mouth. He didn't repeat the sentiment back to me, choosing to enjoy listening to the words rather than repeating them.

My arms circled his neck, and I pressed my tits against his chest, my nipples dragging against his hard muscles as I moved up and down. I pressed my mouth against his and kissed him, my lips trembling as I felt the mouth I fantasized about when he was gone. I took his bottom lip between mine and moaned in his face, my nails cutting into his neck. This was the only man I could ride like this, who had such a big dick that I could be right against him and still enjoy most of his length. I was sitting on top of a warrior, a man with so much power that nothing could ever hurt me again. The head of his cock hit me in the right spot over and over again, and I already felt my thighs shake against his hips. I didn't want to come so soon, but every time I exploded around his dick, it always pleased him.

I rode his dick a little harder, my hips making all the decisions now. I breathed into his mouth because I couldn't kiss him anymore. All I could think about was the small explosion happening between my legs. A cosmic blast that set the world on fire, my orgasm made my hips buck instinctively. I held on to him so I wouldn't slip away, and I moaned right in his face while I enjoyed the amazing things his cock did to me. "Griffin…I love your cock." I'd never been with a man with a more impressive size. Not only was he big, but he knew how to use his size in the best ways possible.

His hands palmed both of my tits, and he flicked his thumb across my nipples, making them pebble in agitation. "He loves you too, baby. You're going to come for me one more time before I fill that pussy. That's how I want to come, watching you come for me."

I pressed my forehead against his and continued to move up and down, my clit dragging against his hard body during my movements. I'd just clenched his dick with my powerful orgasm, but I could feel the arousal course through my body all over again. My nails dug into him, and my pussy smeared his length with my cream. The sexual passion between us was overwhelming, packed with chemistry and insatiable lust. But there was an undeniable connection between us, something even more powerful than this combustive attraction. It was deep and pure, full of love, devotion, and loyalty. Nothing could come between us, not the war between our families, the time we spent apart, or the other men and women who came before us. We were so different, but we fit together so perfectly. This was love, real love. It was the thing that some people searched for their entire lives and never found. But Bones and I had it. We had it the moment we met, even under terrible circumstances. Neither one of us could deny it, and gradually, something very ugly grew into something painfully beautiful.

NINETEEN

Crow
———————

It was hard to believe I was happy just a few hours ago.

My son was living under my roof with his pregnant wife, and I got to see him every day. He was stuck in bed, but I still got to spend lots of time with him. We watched sports, had every meal together, and had conversations deep into the night. I also got to know Sapphire better, and of course, I grew to love my new daughter even more.

My family had avoided death, and I lived every day with gratitude in my heart.

Gratitude for the man who had saved all of us.

Then he pounded on my door and told me off.

Now I sat on the black leather couch in my study, a bottle of aged scotch on the table along with two glasses. The fireplace hadn't been used in months because we were in the hottest part of summer. The curtains were open because the sun was about to set. The gentle light reached the inside of my study, and in a few minutes, I would have to flip on the lights because it was getting too dark.

Button sat across from me, her legs crossed and her lips pressed tightly together. She was having a glass of scotch with me, something she rarely did. When we first met, she didn't drink much, but soon she adapted the Italian ways and drank five glasses of wine every day—at a minimum. But she'd never been a big scotch drinker.

I'd told her everything, every word Griffin said to me.

I mean, *yelled* at me.

Button had her hair pulled over one shoulder, her beautiful brown locks still vibrant in color despite her age. Her face was still gorgeous, despite the gentle crow's-feet in the corners of her eyes and mouth. I saw my daughter when I looked at her, along with my son. Her body still had the signs of childbirth, old scars. But those scars aroused me because she'd given birth to my children. Her body did exceptional things to produce new life. She'd always been a warrior, and becoming a mother was a different way of being a warrior.

She stared at the cold fireplace for a while before her eyes settled on me.

I'd been looking at her the entire time, her face always

giving me a sense of peace. She was the light to my darkness, the hope in my despair. But this time, her qualities couldn't cure the anger sitting in the pit of my stomach.

Button finally said something. "What are you going to do?"

"There's nothing I can do." I grabbed the glass and took a drink, finishing off the scotch before I refilled it. "He meant what he said. It's done." Just when I thought peace had been established between our two families, I realized I was wrong. The past wasn't buried. The resentment and anger still hovered just under the surface. "I guess Vanessa told him about Antonio…and he didn't like what he heard."

"Can you really blame him?" she asked. "I never met him, but Conway told me he's a nice young man. Fully approved of him. You liked him too. Vanessa obviously did as well. If they had more time together…maybe that's who she would have married."

"And he blames me for that." I stared into my glass, looking at the various amber colors within the liquid. "The only way to move forward is for me to apologize… but that's something I can't do." It wasn't because of my pride or stubbornness. I had been protecting my daughter —and I would never apologize for that. "I had every right to do what I did. Any other father would have done the same. So that's not an option. Even if it buried the hatchet, I still wouldn't do it."

She crossed her arms over her chest as she looked at me. "I understand. But let's not forget what this man did for us. He saved our son. He saved you. He saved Cane and Sapphire. We owe this man everything."

I would never forget what he did. It wasn't something I would ever sweep under the rug. "I'll never apologize for something without meaning it. I did apologize to him for the way I treated him, for my cruelty. But I won't apologize for doing the right thing for my daughter. I won't take back what I said, what I did."

"I don't think an apology would make a difference anyway. It doesn't change the past."

"Then what the hell does he want?" I took another drink and slammed the glass onto the table. The only thing he wanted was my daughter, and I gave it to him. Despite the way he lit into me, I wouldn't interfere with his relationship with my daughter. I would tolerate him because I was indebted to him for the rest of my life. It was a small price to pay for what he did for me, saving my only son's life.

"Maybe he doesn't want anything," she said calmly. "Maybe he's just hurt. Maybe he's just heartbroken. Maybe he doesn't know how else to channel that pain. Maybe yelling at you gave him closure on what happened."

"No. I think it opened the hostility again."

"Think about it." She scooted to the edge of the cushion and rested her arms on her knees. "Vanessa is the closest thing he's ever had to family. He resented her for the life she had. He wanted to kill us because of the life we took away from him. And then you did it again when you took away Vanessa."

I wasn't following her. "What's your point, Button?"

"He's a very strong man. He's very powerful and successful. He doesn't strike me as the kind of man who expresses a lot of emotions. But this is something that has always haunted him, that's always bothered him."

"What, exactly?" I asked.

"Family," she whispered. "He doesn't have a family. He doesn't have somewhere he belongs. Maybe he doesn't even understand that's what's missing, but it clearly is. He's angry at you because you took his mother and father away. Then you took Vanessa. You keep taking everything away from him, and he can't stand it anymore. He doesn't want you to have that power over him. He wants you to…"

"What?" I asked.

"He wants to be part of our family."

"As in, he wants to marry my daughter?" I asked, not following Button's thought process.

"Well, yes. But that's not what I mean. Crow, when I first

came here, I was scared. I was in a foreign place, and I just wanted to go home. But as I grew comfortable here with you and Cane, I realized there was nothing waiting for me back home. You became my family. Cane became my family. And then we made our family grow."

I understood that well. I understood that I gave my wife everything she'd been missing. When we had Conway, she told me that her life finally felt complete, that she filled the void she'd been carrying around. Once she became a Barsetti, she finally found the place where she belonged.

"He wants to be part of our family, Crow."

I dropped my gaze and looked into the scotch again. "I told him I accepted him for my daughter. I shook his hand. I thought we moved on. Why is that not enough?"

"Accepting someone is the bare minimum, Crow. Make him feel like he belongs here."

I squeezed the glass, wanting to shatter it. "I'll never forget what he did for our family, but let's not forget what he did to Vanessa. Let's not forget the reason we hated him in the first place."

"People change, Crow. I think he's proven to us that he's not the man we once despised. He's proven that love changed him, that Vanessa made him into a great man. The two of you are a lot alike…whether you choose to see it or not."

I finished the glass before I set it on the table. I didn't deny her claim, knowing the similarities were striking. Griffin and I both were hard criminals who only turned soft when we found the right woman. There was no doubt in my mind that he wasn't a threat to my family, that he would treat Vanessa right and protect her. But I refused to admit that fact out loud.

"You can't apologize for what you did. But you can move forward and change the relationship."

"Button, I don't think he wants a relationship with me. He made his feelings for me very clear…"

"It won't happen overnight. It'll take time. But you need to start somewhere."

I didn't even know where to begin. I didn't know how to talk to him. I didn't know how to relate to him. It was easy with my kids because I'd raised them. They were younger versions of Button and me.

"Crow." Button kept her blue eyes on me.

I met her look, my jaw tight.

"If you want to make this right, that's what you need to do. After what he's done for us…I think he's earned it. It'll finally end the blood war for good, and we can start a new chapter."

If someone told me that my greatest enemy's son would be part of my life, I would have said that wasn't possible.

If someone told me he would love my daughter, I would have refused to believe that. It was reality, but even now, it was still hard to believe.

"We all need to make him feel welcome in this family," Button said. "But it needs to start with you."

TWENTY

Bones
_____

When I woke up that morning, I rolled on top of
Vanessa, fucked her, and then got out of bed. I did my
workout in the living room, hopped in the shower, and
then sat at the kitchen table in my sweatpants while I read
the newspaper. A mug of hot coffee sat on the table in
front of me, and I sipped it as the sunlight slowly filled the
apartment with the rising sun. Now that the painting was
out of our lives, I finally felt comfortable in the space.
The painting she replaced it with was one she'd made
of me.

I hadn't had a chance to ask her about it yet.

A few hours later, Vanessa woke up and joined me. She
usually grabbed whatever t-shirt I left behind and threw it
on, looking sexy as hell in my oversized clothes. Her footsteps sounded against the hardwood floor as she
approached me from behind. When she stopped behind

me, she wrapped her arms around my chest, leaned down, and then peppered my shoulder with kisses.

I dropped the paper on the table and hooked my arm across hers until I gripped her hand. I watched her kiss me, her long hair trailing down my chest and tickling my skin. Her smell wrapped around me, the hint of shampoo and perfume. The grin stretched across my face, treasuring the moment to keep forever. This was what I wanted for the rest of my life, just the two of us, living a simple life. "Morning."

"Morning." She pressed her mouth against mine and kissed me. She gave my chest and shoulders a squeeze before she stood straight and walked fully into the kitchen.

My eyes moved to her ass, wishing my long shirt didn't cover it. Her pussy was full of the seed I put there a few hours ago, and I wanted to look at my handiwork. She didn't like to wake up as early as I did, so she always went right back to sleep once I was finished. With warm come inside her, she dozed off for another few hours while I worked out and made breakfast.

"Did you already eat?" She pulled a bowl from the cabinet along with a box of cereal.

"Yes."

"I was going to offer to make you some cereal." She poured the milk into the bowl and grabbed a spoon.

I cocked an eyebrow, full of amusement. "Make me cereal? Baby, you can't make cereal."

She carried the bowl to the table and sat down. She crossed her legs then dug her spoon into the bowl. "I beg to differ. This is one of my favorite recipes."

I preferred to have a woman who could cook, but I loved Vanessa just the way she was. She could fight like a man and paint like a master, but she couldn't work a set of pans if her life depended on it. "Not a recipe."

"It has two ingredients," she argued. "That's enough evidence."

I turned back to my paper again, the grin still on my mouth.

"I like it when you smile."

My eyes moved back up to look at her, and once I saw the affection in her eyes, I dropped my smile. "You haven't seen me smile enough to know if you like it."

"Just seeing it once is enough for me." She smiled at me before she turned back to her cereal.

Now I didn't care about the paper anymore. All I wanted to do was look at her, look at those pretty eyes and those full lips.

She kept eating like she didn't notice my look. "We should go see my family sometime today. I told them I would come by for dinner, but that didn't happen. I'll give them a call after I shower."

I never told her I'd screamed at her father. My temper got the best of me, and I torched the new relationship we'd finally established. But after everything that man put me through, I didn't regret it. Vanessa could have ended up with another man because of his decision. She should be with me—end of story. I didn't like her father, and I would never like him. I didn't expect him to like me when we first met, but I expected him to keep an open mind considering he wasn't always the honorable man he is now. But he never gave me a chance. He was determined to destroy me right from the beginning. I'd proven myself a million times over, so now I didn't need his approval. All I wanted was Vanessa, and now that I had her, I didn't give a damn about him.

When I didn't say anything, she looked at me. "Is that okay?"

"Yes." Her family was important to her, so I would go through the motions to make her happy. I wasn't sure if I should tell her I yelled at her father, or if I should give Crow the honor of telling her. It seemed awkward no matter how we confessed. Since he hadn't said a single word or given me any kind of response, I had no idea how he felt about my speech. He didn't punch me, so I guess he wasn't that mad about it. If he ratted on me, I would know the answer—and respect him even less.

Just when I turned back to my paper, there was a knock on the door.

My eyes flicked back up and looked at her. "Expecting someone?"

She finished chewing her food as she raised her eyebrows. "No."

If it was the painter, I'd punch him so hard he'd fly down the stairs. I set my paper down and rose to my feet.

"It's okay," she said. "I'll get—"

"No." My authority burned through my gaze as I stared at her, my look keeping her pinned into her seat. "I'm the one who answers the door—not you." I walked across the apartment and approached the front door, unsure who I would be faced with. It was eleven in the morning, too early for a random visitor. I opened the door and came face-to-face with the worst possible person.

Crow.

In a black t-shirt with dark jeans, he looked exactly the same as the last time I saw him. With his tanned skin and masculine features, he was still a good-looking man despite his age. He carried himself like a soldier ready for battle, his muscle tone still impressive because he lifted weights every day of his life. He could never compare to me, not when I had thirty years of youth on my side. We both knew that bullet would have killed him. My strength and vigor were greater, so I survived.

I kept my hand on the knob as I stared at him, watching him stare back at me with the same cryptic expression. I was shirtless and in my sweatpants, my hair slightly messy from rolling around in bed with his daughter, but I wasn't ashamed of it. I was fucking his daughter every night, but I was also loving her, protecting her, and being the man she deserved.

I thought of the last words I said to him.

Fuck. You.

He hadn't said anything at the time, but maybe he was ready to say something now.

"Is this a bad time?" His words were anticlimactic. I expected more from him, a fist to the mouth or an insult to the ears.

"No. I'll get Vanessa." I turned my back on him, letting him look at all the ink I had all over my body. He hadn't seen me shirtless before, so now he knew I was completely covered with the skulls, dragons, bullets, and gravestones.

"I'm not here for her."

I turned back around, my muscles naturally flexing in preparation for a fight. His calmness only made me more suspicious. A part of me wanted him to finally snap and start a fight. I wanted an excuse to hit him, but he had to make the first move—otherwise, it would be a betrayal to Vanessa. "Then what do you want?" If he wanted to continue this conversation on my doorstep, it was tacky. I was handicapped with my woman in the next room.

He still didn't seem angry, and there wasn't a gun on his hip or tucked inside his waistband. "A drink—if you're free."

He wanted to get a drink with me? It wasn't too early to hit a bar, not for someone like me. I started drinking as soon as I finished my coffee, and that was around nine in the morning. The only reason I hadn't already had a glass of scotch was because of my woman. She'd asked me to cut back—and I listened. With her by my side, I didn't need it anyway, not the way I used to. "A drink?" I asked blankly.

"Yes. It's not too early, right?" He moved his hands into his pockets. "I know we both start before lunch."

Most of the time when I was with Crow, he was drinking scotch. It didn't matter what time of day it was. The only time he seemed to drink wine was when he was with his family. It made me wonder if he even liked it.

He must want to talk about the last conversation we had, but I didn't think there was anything left to say. "I meant what I said. I won't apologize for it. You stand by every decision you made until this point. Let's just leave it alone."

His expression didn't change. He used to wear his rage on his face, silently threatening me with his dark eyes full of malice. But now he was a conundrum, impossible to read. He must have done that on purpose. "That's fine. I still want that drink."

Then what the hell did he want to talk about?

"I'll wait for you on the sidewalk." He took the steps back down then faced the road, his hands still in his pockets.

I finally shut the door and walked back inside.

"Who was that?" Vanessa asked from the table.

"Your father."

She pushed away her bowl of soggy cereal. "Really? Why didn't you invite him inside?"

"Because you're practically naked."

She looked down at herself, seeing my t-shirt barely hiding her pointed nipples and blue thong.

"And he wants to get a drink."

She glanced at the time on the microwave. "It's not even noon."

"Yes, I know it's late."

She narrowed her eyes on my face, not appreciating the joke. "I'll get dressed, then."

"He says he's here for me, not you."

She was about to rise out of her chair but lowered herself instead. "Oh…that's nice."

She had no idea that it wasn't nice at all. He obviously had an agenda. I was about to find out what it was. "I'll be back in an hour or so. Where will you be?" I wanted to know where my woman was at every moment. She was officially mine, and I wanted her to be safe at all times. I had a beautiful woman to guard—and I took my job very seriously.

"I'll shower then work at the gallery. I haven't been open in so long…hopefully, I still have customers."

With her kind of talent, she could close down for a year, and there would still be business. "You will, baby."

———

THE WALK to the bar was the most awkward five minutes of my life.

We walked side by side, not making small talk. With our eyes glued to our destination, we kept as much space between us as possible. He didn't want to be any closer to me than he had to be, and that feeling was mutual.

We walked inside the bar and got a booth in the corner. There were only a few customers there at that time of day since it was during a weekday, and lunchtime hadn't even arrived.

We ordered our drinks, both scotch, and then faced each other.

Crow held my gaze without backing down, but he seemed disgruntled, like he didn't want to be there at all.

Neither did I. I'd rather be at home with Vanessa, watching her paint in the living room or do the dishes in the kitchen. Everything she did was fascinating to me. When she concentrated on her work, she bit her bottom lip from time to time. Sometimes she would mouth words to a song under her breath, but she wouldn't actually sing. I always wondered if she sang only when she was alone.

Our drinks arrived, and we both snatched the glasses and got the amber liquid down our throats as quickly as possible. We went straight for the hard liquor, skipping the beer and wine unlike everyone else in that bar.

Silence passed. It seemed to last a lifetime.

I wasn't sure why he'd dragged me down here if he had nothing to say.

Unintimidated, I held his gaze and waited, refusing to speak first. He was the one who disturbed my day. He was the one who pulled me from Vanessa—again. This was the kind of bullshit I would have to deal with for the rest of my life, an overprotective father who wouldn't back off.

If I didn't love my baby so damn much…

He finally said something. "You're right, I'm not going to apologize for the things I've done. I won't apologize for taking my daughter away from you. I'll never apologize for protecting my little girl…even if she's not a little girl anymore."

"Thank you for dragging me all the way down here to tell me that."

He ignored the sarcastic jab. "I accept your hatred. In your eyes, I've earned it. That's fine with me. I won't lose any sleep over it."

"Just as arrogant as ever."

His eyes narrowed. "As are you."

I drank from my glass, not denying it.

"We can't change the past, and I'm sure neither of us wants to change it anyway. My reasons for hating you were valid. Your reasons for hating me are also valid. But I would like to put it behind us and move forward. Since you're no longer the same man, your past is irrelevant. I'm willing to forget about it because you've proven how much you love my daughter. I've come to realize we're very similar. I wasn't a good man until I met the woman I love…and you have the same story."

He wanted us to bury the past and start over, but for me, that wasn't an option. "Look, I'm willing to put on a show for Vanessa because it makes her happy. I'll live in Florence so she can see you all the time, I'll come over for family dinners and shake your hand, I'll give your wife a hug and make small talk with Conway. But let's leave it at that. Let's not be in the same room together any longer than that. We're just wasting time when we would both rather be doing something else." Maybe he felt guilty about the bullet I took for him. Maybe he felt like he owed me more because of the sacrifice I made. "All I want is Vanessa. Now that I have her, I don't want anything else. So you don't need to make this gesture out of obligation. I didn't save your life for you—I did it for her." I took another drink, letting the warm liquid fill my stomach.

He swirled his glass slightly before he looked into the liquid. It was the first time he'd dropped his gaze, abruptly ended contact with me. Maybe he felt relieved by what I said. Or maybe he felt something else entirely. "I'm not sitting here out of obligation or guilt. I'm not sitting here for Vanessa. I'm sitting here because I misjudged you, Griffin." He set his glass down and looked me in the eye again. "I understand you want nothing to do with me, but I want to get to know you. I want a relationship with you."

I couldn't believe my ears. The Crow Barsetti I knew would never say anything like that. The only time I ever heard him say anything heartfelt was when he spoke to

Vanessa. I stared at him blankly, unsure if I should be annoyed or disappointed. "Is this a joke?"

"No." He looked me in the eye, his voice not shaking. "Conway married Sapphire, and now she's a daughter to me. Instead of losing a son, I've gained another Barsetti. I know you'll never be a Barsetti, but you will be my son-in-law. But I want you to be more than that…I want you to be my son."

I still couldn't believe any of this. "When I called you to tell you about Conway being captured, you threatened to kill me." That was just a few weeks ago, not ancient history like he was pretending it was.

He winced slightly.

"And you told me I was trash and I always would be trash. Why the fuck would you want trash to be part of your family?"

He winced again, soaking in the words I threw back at him.

"Your insults don't wound me. Bullets don't even wound me. But let's not pretend—"

"I'm not pretending I never said those things, Griffin. I said them, and I meant them—at the time. But I realize I was wrong. You've proven me wrong, Griffin. You're not trash. You're a very powerful and admirable man. When you ask my permission to marry my daughter, I will gladly give it to you."

"Ask your permission?" I asked with a snort. "No, asshole. I will not ask for your permission. I earned that shit when I took that bullet for you. I never have to ask you for anything else."

He dropped his gaze again, but this time, his breathing was different. He rubbed his temple then looked out the window, his hard appearance softening right before my eyes. Minutes passed, and he didn't say anything.

I looked away, hoping this ridiculous conversation was over.

He turned back to me a short while later. "Griffin."

I met his gaze, swallowing my annoyance.

"Please don't take that away from me." He placed his hand over his heart. "Please let me give my daughter away. Please let me be involved. Please show me the ring and tell me when you're going to ask my daughter to be your wife. I understand if you don't care or think it's important...but it means the world to me."

It was my turn to look away, uncomfortable with the emotion on his face. He never showed vulnerability in front of me, and the reason it bothered me so much was because I could feel his pain. I could feel his emotion...

and it made me care. Unable to form a response verbally, I only gave a nod.

He dropped his hand and breathed a sigh of relief. "Thank you, Griffin."

I drank from my glass then waved down the bartender for another. I hated myself for caring about his feelings, for caving to his plea so easily. In my heart, I knew I didn't do that for Vanessa. I did it out of respect…because he was a good father. I never doubted how much he loved Vanessa and Conway. I never doubted how much he loved his wife. It was one of the reasons I hated him so much…that he had something I never did.

The bartender brought new glasses then walked away.

I continued to stare at my drink, not wanting to look at Crow's face anymore.

"I don't expect things to change overnight. I don't expect you to even like me. And if you never like me, that's fine. But either way, I want to be part of your life. I want my own relationship with you, to get to know the man I've come to admire and respect."

My eyes lifted to his face, to see the sincerity in his gaze.

"I'm not the kind of man who admits when he's wrong because I'm never wrong. But with you…I was very wrong. You've proven your loyalty and your love. I trust you implicitly. I'm very happy to know my daughter has you. That's all a father wants, for his daughter to marry a good man. You're a good man, Griffin."

The only other person who'd ever said that to me was Vanessa…that I was a good man.

Crow stared at me for a long time, as if he expected me to say something.

I didn't have any words. Even without knowing Crow as well as Vanessa did, I knew I could assume this was challenging for him. For him to sit down with his enemy's son and try to start a relationship couldn't have been easy, and no one could make him do it either. Not only was this genuine, but also difficult. After everything he did to me, it was hard for me not to hate him, and it was even harder for me to stand his company like this. But something he said sank into my skin, hit the right nerve.

When I didn't say anything, Crow spoke again. "Tell me something about yourself."

"I'm not very interesting." I wasn't trying to be difficult, but that was the truth.

"I never assumed you were." A slight smile moved onto his lips, telling me he was joking. "Tell me anything about yourself."

I couldn't believe I was sitting across from Crow Barsetti in a bar in Florence, having a casual conversation like friendly acquaintances. This man had been my father's enemy for decades, and he was the reason I was orphaned before I was even ten years old. Now, I was in love with his daughter, forging a strange bond between us because we loved the same woman. "I'm not much of a talker."

"Neither am I."

"Then this should be fun..." I looked away, a sigh escaping my lips.

He drank from his glass, still looking at me. "Come on, meet me halfway."

When I chuckled, it was full of anger. "I tried to meet you halfway once before..."

"You've proven you're the bigger man. So do it again."

I wasn't used to this kind of flattery from anyone but Vanessa.

"Alright." He swirled his scotch like it was wine. "I'll go first." He cleared his throat. "When that thug had his gun pointed at me, I was scared. I've had a gun pointed between my eyes like that many times, but it was always without a hint of fear."

"You didn't look scared to me."

"I'm the best bluffer I know."

"Why were you scared that time but not the others?" Now that we were talking about something interesting, I stopped focusing on the awkward situation that existed from the two of us being together.

"Because every other time I've been held at gunpoint, my family has been safe. One time, I was being tortured in a warehouse because this asshole wanted my wife. He demanded that I give up her location. She was pregnant with Conway at the time. Of course, he was wasting his time." He shifted his gaze out the window, the memory dancing across his eyes. "He cocked the gun and prepared to pull the trigger. But I didn't care…because my wife and son were safe. In Milan, that wasn't the case. I did the best I could to save my son. I thought I could blow out the engine so Conway could run, but that didn't happen. I fell to the ground, a failure. And that was why I was scared… because my son wasn't safe."

I held my glass but kept my eyes on him, seeing the picture he painted with his words. I remembered seeing him on the ground, staring down the barrel of the gun. He took his death with dignity, not giving his executioner any power over him. I'd killed a lot of men, and most of them went out like a pussy. They pretended to be brave until things got real, until they were held at gunpoint. Then they pissed themselves. Shit themselves. Begged for their lives. Crow Barsetti didn't do that. He was a strong man, and it didn't surprise me that he raised such a strong daughter.

When I didn't speak, Crow kept talking. "I raised my son

to be the strongest man he could possibly be, and I think I succeeded. But he was ambushed without any warning, and there was nothing he could do but hope that someone would rescue him. I won't be around forever. I won't always be there to save him. Sapphire won't be able to protect him because she takes care of him in other ways. But you will be there...and that brings me peace. Before I knew you were dating my daughter, I told her I wanted her to marry a powerful man. It didn't matter if he was rich because money can cause more problems than it solves sometimes. I'm not clueless to my daughter's special qualities, and I can confidently say she can have any man she wants...and she's chosen you. All I wanted was someone who could protect her when I'm gone. You fit the bill perfectly." He took another drink, handling his liquor just as well as I did even though I was thirty years younger than him.

"No one will ever bother her as long as I live." I said it with complete confidence, meaning every single word. A man would never get within ten feet of her without being chased off. I would be the guard dog by her side. All I would do was growl, and men would shit themselves.

He gave a slight nod. "I believe you. That's all Pearl and I want."

"Well, you're getting your wish."

He gave another slight nod. "Does that mean you'll be quitting the business?"

"Are you going to point a gun at my head if I say no?" Our conversation was going well, but I couldn't restrain myself from these vicious comments. For the past eight months, this man had dictated my life completely. My relationship with Vanessa revolved around him like he was the damn sun. He bossed me around and laid down all the rules.

He sighed while wearing a small smile. "No. I was only curious."

"And nosy."

He clenched his jaw almost imperceptibly, swallowing the frustration my words caused. "My daughter is an adult and I will respect her privacy, but one thing will never change. I will always look after her, even when I'm eighty and she's closing in on fifty. I won't deny that I want you to walk away from that life. After what happened with Conway, let's learn from his mistake. The best way to guarantee a peaceful life is to live a peaceful life."

I didn't think my occupation would interfere with Vanessa's safety. We were careful to hide our organization, to never show our faces. Work and pleasure were distinctly different.

"So…are you?"

My eyes narrowed in annoyance before I took a drink. "I'm not worried about something bad happening to Vanessa because of my job. But every time I leave her, it kills me inside. She's worried about me the entire time, counting down the minutes until I'm safe again. I've decided to quit because I can't put her through that every few weeks. I don't want my woman staying with her parents every time I'm gone. She feels the safest with me...so I'll be there every night." Vanessa and I had discussed having a family. She gave me an ultimatum and said if I wanted to be with her, I had to become a father. I didn't want to have kids, but since it was a requirement in order to be with her, I caved. And if that was in our future, then I definitely couldn't have that kind of job anymore. I couldn't leave my woman and my children unprotected for weeks at a time.

Crow didn't hide the relief on his face. "I'm glad to hear that."

"I have to help out with a few more things before I leave, so I have a couple more missions. But once they're completed, it'll be over."

Crow didn't hide his displeasure, but he also didn't make an argument about it. "When did you get into that line of work?"

"In my early twenties. I met Max and the rest of the boys on the streets. We needed money, so our operation started small, like stealing cars and robbing houses. It slowly grew into the business it is now."

Crow nodded but didn't pass judgment on my career choice. "Is it something you enjoy?"

"Yes." I wasn't ashamed to say that. "The men we hit aren't good men. From sex trafficking to murder, these men are guilty of a lot of terrible things. Men pay us to destroy their enemies, but enemies like that are usually the bad guys."

Crow swished his drink. "When I was your age, I lived for that sort of thing. Since I wasn't responsible for anyone else, my life wasn't valuable. Therefore, it didn't matter whether I lived or died. There was no risk. I traded arms with all kinds of men, giving them weapons of mass destruction. Knowing full well those guns would kill other people, I sold them for a profit. I was exactly as you are now when I was your age…until I met my wife. At that moment, everything changed. I didn't like who she turned me into. I didn't like how she changed my priorities. I didn't like how she made me feel. Eventually, the changes became so drastic that I couldn't remember who I used to be."

That was exactly how I felt about myself. "I know what you mean."

"My wife told me we're a lot alike… She was right." He chuckled before he took a drink. "That woman is always right."

"So is Vanessa."

"That doesn't surprise me. She got her mother's strength and intelligence. She got my stubbornness."

"And your punch, your aim, and your reflexes." Vanessa was a strong woman, born of two remarkable parents. She wasn't the weak damsel-in-distress I met time after time. Most women I met just wanted someone to tell them what to do, to have someone look after them because they didn't know how to look after themselves. Vanessa was nothing like that.

Crow smiled slightly. "Yes, she did."

"I still don't like you, but I admire you for raising her. I don't think I would have fallen in love with anyone else but her." I'd paid whores to fulfill my fantasies, and I'd picked up women at the bar purely for sex. Women were sexual objects. They weren't people I could actually relate to. But then I'd met a woman who shook the ground underneath my feet.

"Thank you," he said, showing a hint of pride in his eyes.

"What was she like? Growing up?"

Crow played with the glass between his fingertips as he reflected on her younger years. "Pretty much the same as she is now. She constantly questioned the world around her. If a teacher told her to do an assignment one way, she would question it and do it a different way. When she got a bad mark for the assignment, she wouldn't get angry about it. She understood marks didn't really matter, that understanding there were better ways of doing things was what really mattered. She was very wise for her age. But she always had an attitude. She always had sass. And one time, she beat up a kid at school because he lifted her dress."

I smiled, immensely proud of the younger version of Vanessa that I never knew. "How old was she?"

Crow paused as he thought about it. "Nine or so."

"Good."

He chuckled. "She got in trouble for it. She received a much harder punishment for the violence than the boy did for lifting her dress. Of course, that made her angry, so she asked us to challenge the school's policy. Her punishment had already been served, but that didn't matter to her. She wanted justice for what happened, but she also wanted to the change the protocol for the future. In her eyes, she was being discouraged from standing up for herself. The only other possibility would be to allow the boy to keep doing it until someone heard her screams and came to help her. She said that wasn't the way girls should be taught, to scream and wait for someone to help them. They should be taught to fight, to protect them- selves and not be submissive for fear of punishment."

I set my glass down, my mind numb from what I'd just heard. "She said all of this when she was nine?"

He nodded, the pride on his face undeniable. "Yes."

I shook my head, a smile on my lips. "Fucking badass."

"I know. She was always a smart girl. Always a champion. Her personality and morals never changed as she got older. I was always protective of her when it came to boys, always present and rarely allowing her to be alone with one."

"You don't say…"

He gave a guilty shrug. "But Vanessa was so smart I never really had to worry about it. When she went off to college on her own, I knew she was a grown woman and I didn't need to worry about her anymore. She had good instincts, and she would explore romantic relationships with men… because that's what she was supposed to do. But then she brought you home…and I forgot all the credibility she'd previously established with me. I didn't trust her at all, blind to my own hatred. I forgot how smart and strong my daughter was…and I never really listened to her. That was my fault."

When another insult came to my lips, I swallowed it back. Listening to him describe his daughter with such pride softened my anger. I knew he always tried to do the best thing for her, tried to protect her but strengthen her at the same time. So I swallowed back the retort and let it go.

"It seems like the best thing we have in common is Vanessa—we both love her."

I nodded. "True."

"What is your favorite thing about her?"

My answer changed depending on what time of day it was. If it was early in the morning or late at night, my favorite thing about her was her naked body, the beautiful slit between her legs. Her gorgeous tits as they pointed at the ceiling while she lay on her back. That was my favorite thing about her, having her pinned against my mattress while I enjoyed her like I owned her—which I did. I told Vanessa she had to pay the price for the sacrifice I'd made by becoming mine forever. She could never leave even if she stopped loving me. She was a possession now, not just my lover. "It's hard to narrow it down just to one thing. But when I think of the moment when I fell for her, it has to be her fierceness. I'm three times her size and terrifying enough to make grown men shit their pants. But she didn't hesitate to fight me, to outsmart me whenever the opportunity presented itself. She didn't think twice before she grabbed that gun, pointed it right at my heart, and pulled the trigger. She meant to kill me. I saw it in her eyes." When I thought of that night, I felt the coldness against my fingertips, the frozen air as it entered my lungs. I could still hear the crunch of the snow underneath my boots. I could even see the vapor escape my mouth when I breathed. I remembered that night with clarity because it was the night that changed my life forever.

"Isn't that the night you met her?" he asked.

"Yes." I wasn't a romantic guy. I had no experience with love, not even when I was young. But when I met Vanessa on that winter night, the feeling in my chest was undeniable. I thought I just wanted to fuck her, but when I looked back over our relationship, I knew that was the beginning of something much deeper. "I fell in love with her the night I met her. I just didn't realize it at the time."

Crow watched my expression as he held on to his glass, surveying the different emotions that danced across my gaze. "I'm going to tell you something that only my brother knows. I'll share it with you if you keep it a secret, especially from Vanessa. I know I can trust you."

I gave a slight nod.

"Pearl had been your father's prisoner for a long time, about three months. Cane and I only stole her because she seemed to be the one thing your father cared about. At the time, I had no idea about your mom. He must have kept her a secret on purpose. So, I stole Pearl to get revenge. I intended to rape her and kill her." He spoke about his horrible intentions without skipping a beat.

I didn't react at all, not surprised.

"When she was in my possession, she fought my men with a kind of battle rage I've never seen. She punched, stabbed, did everything she could to get away. I cornered her like a wild animal, and she was about to turn the knife on herself. She was willing to kill herself because being a prisoner for another moment was unbearable. I respected her for it, respected her for fighting as hard as she could until she realized there was no way out."

I imagined a younger version of Pearl holding the point of a knife against her stomach. I imagined the moment they met each other, not seeing a hint of romance there.

"I got the knife from her, and instead of being cruel to her like I should have been, I asked her permission to put a syringe in her neck and put her to sleep. Instead of leaving her at the base, I took her back to my house... where we both live now. Long story short, I couldn't rape her like I planned. I couldn't beat her like I planned. I respected her way too much...admired her way too much. I wished that my sister had that same kind of fight, that she hadn't given up. So I bargained with Pearl for her freedom. I told her if she worked off a jar of buttons by pleasing me, I would let her go. It's not any better than raping her, not when I leveraged her freedom against her in exchange for fucking."

I listened to every word, transfixed by the story. He really was the biggest hypocrite I'd ever heard of.

"I think I fell in love with her that first time we interacted, when she killed one of my men and fought until the very end. When she was in my captivity, she still fought me constantly, not just with her fists, but her words. I respected her...she forced me to respect her...and that made me love her. Our stories are very similar..."

"Identical."

He nodded.

"You're the biggest hypocrite on the planet."

He shrugged. "I won't deny it. And I won't apologize for wanting more for my daughter. Now that you know this, you can run off to Vanessa and tell her. You can turn her against me. You can drive a wedge between us so you don't have to deal with me all the time. I'm giving you power over me…just as I had so much power over you."

It was tempting. I'd been punished for committing the same crimes he committed. He kept me away from the woman I loved for months, put me in mortal agony. But the idea of getting my revenge wasn't appealing…not this time. He confided something to me that he didn't have to tell me. Just as I gave him a loaded shotgun when we first met, he gave me a loaded gun in return. But these bullets could really destroy him.

He stared at me as he waited for a response.

"There's nothing I could ever say to Vanessa to turn her against you."

His eyes softened.

"She loves you. She loves all of you more than anything else in the world…even me. So you never have to worry about your daughter turning her back on you. Her love is unconditional. I never hear her say anything about bad about any of you, and when I say I think you're the biggest asshole on the planet, she tells me not to talk about you that way."

His eyes softened even more, turning emotional in a way he only did for his daughter.

"But I will take your secret to the grave, Crow. I don't want to rip her family apart. I've never wanted that. I love her too damn much to ever cause her pain. She needs you to be happy."

"She needs you too," he whispered. "I'm sorry it took me so long to realize that."

I didn't accept his apology. It would be a while before I was ready. "Are you going to tell her I screamed at you?" I stormed to his front door and practically broke it down when I knocked. When I yelled at him, I didn't give him a chance to say anything. I just told him he was lower than trash and I didn't care whether he lived or died. I meant every single word I said, and even now I hadn't apologized for it. If he told Vanessa, she wouldn't leave me, but I knew she wouldn't be happy about it.

He leaned forward with his elbows resting on the table, his glass cupped between both of his hands. He considered my question for nearly a minute, his eyes flicking back and forth between me and his glass. "I'll take it to the grave."

TWENTY-ONE

Mia

He said he would never let me go.

Never.

After everything I'd been through, settling for living in a beautiful mansion near Verona didn't sound so bad. After being cruelly treated for so long, I was exhausted. I didn't have faith in people anymore.

That belief died a long time ago.

It would be easy to give up, to hang myself from the bedpost in the bedroom.

It was very tempting.

But I had one thing to live for, one thing I couldn't give up on.

Never.

So I had to come up with a plan. I either had to kill him or run away.

Even though he said he would never let me go, the idea of killing him didn't seem right. He said I could eat whenever I wanted, and as long as I didn't provoke him, he never laid a hand on me. He was attracted to me, wanted a reason to get between my legs, but he never acted on it.

This guy was a god compared to the devil I used to live with.

Egor deserved death, not Carter.

That gave me one alternative.

To run.

I had a tracker in my ankle, and I was stuck in a mansion with an alarm system and a wall that surrounded the property. The wall wasn't an issue. With adrenaline pumping in my veins, climbing over that thing wouldn't slow me down. Even the alarm system wouldn't stop me, not if I timed it right. If I did it in the dead of night when he was asleep, I could make it out the front door and over the wall before he could catch up. In the darkness, I could run or hide somewhere. With the countryside on either side of us, I had a good chance.

Or better yet, I could take one of his cars. I could dismantle all the others so he couldn't come after me.

It was an elaborate plan, but I could pull it off if I took my time.

I had to make sure this worked. If I didn't, Carter would make good on his threat.

He would hurt me and fuck me—like he promised.

It would be nothing like being with Egor, that was obvious. Egor was just cruel. Carter was a good-looking man, a man so confident that he could subdue me without hurting me. His words were enough. He was the king of this palace, and he ruled so effortlessly. Fucking him wouldn't be the worst, not when he had the body of a god and the face of a model. If we'd met under different circumstances, I would gladly get under him.

That lowered the risk significantly.

Because if I didn't make it out…I could deal with the consequences.

I walked into the kitchen that morning and found Carter sitting at the dining table, the sunlight filtering through the windows and bringing heat into the room. Shirtless and in just his sweatpants, he looked the same as he did every morning. With messy hair, a beard growing in, and lazy eyes, he sat with the newspaper in his hands. A cup of coffee was beside him.

He didn't have any breakfast because he expected me to cook for him—every morning.

I stepped out of the kitchen, my arms crossed over my chest. I wore the jeans and t-shirt he'd provided for me, my hair pulled into a braid over one shoulder. "Do you ever wear a shirt?" Unless he left the house, he always paraded around half naked. His body was perfect, and he obviously wasn't ashamed of the chiseled muscles of his chest and torso. With his strength and tanned skin, he possessed the kind of fitness that suggested he worked out on a regular basis. I had no idea when those sessions occurred because I'd never seen them.

He wasn't startled by my unannounced presence. His eyes kept scanning his paper. "Too distracting for you?"

I rolled my eyes.

He grinned like he knew what I'd just done. "My door is always open, sweetheart. Just let me know." He looked up from his paper, wearing the most arrogant grin I'd ever seen. "You can hop on my lap right now."

I rolled my eyes again, exaggerating my movements so he could see how sincere it was. "What do you want for breakfast?"

"You." He set the paper down and dropped his smile, looking at me with an intensity that would frighten anyone.

I'd have been more scared if I didn't know he wouldn't rush me and pin me against the wall.

He kept up his stare, not blinking or even moving. His broad shoulders covered the back of the chair, and even without a crown, he still possessed the kind of power only a member of the nobility would have. When he looked at me like that, his stare was even more invasive than Egor's bare touch. Carter could touch me without placing a hand on my skin. He could invade me easily, getting inside my mind with just his confidence.

I refused to let him believe he could get under my skin, so I turned around and walked into the kitchen. "The usual, it is." Once the wall separated us, I finally took a deep breath and dropped my stern expression. This man made me walk on eggshells without actually doing anything to me. It was a different kind of presence. When Egor didn't get his way, he resorted to torture to make me cooperate. But this man didn't need to resort to such measures.

"You're blushing."

"Jesus." I nearly jumped out of my skin, not noticing him standing there. He must have walked into the room quietly, or I was so distracted I hadn't noticed him. My hand flew to my chest, feeling my erratic heartbeat under the skin.

He gripped the edge of the counter on the other side of the island, staring at me with the same fierce expression he wore in the dining room.

"Is there something you wanted?"

He cocked his head slightly, his eyes narrowing a little more. "You look like a strawberry right now. A cute strawberry. I wonder if your pussy is the same color."

My eyes widened to the size of baseballs, and my jaw nearly hit the floor. "Keep it up, and you won't be getting breakfast at all."

"That's fine by me. I already said I preferred you."

He was digging his way under my skin, making my breath uneven and shallow. He was burying himself deep, like a knife cutting through muscle and bone. I couldn't let it affect me, couldn't give him any indication that I really was blushing…everywhere. I turned to the fridge and grabbed the carton of eggs. "I'll make you what I made yesterday, then." I grabbed my supplies and set them on the counter, doing my best to ignore him.

He hovered there, still staring at me with the intimate expression. As long as he stood there, my cheeks would continue to burn the color of rubies. Something about his presence unnerved me, not the way Egor's did. I didn't feel unsafe in that moment. I felt something else entirely.

I cleared my throat. "Yes?"

He moved around the corner, and just when I thought he was going to leave the room, he came around the kitchen island.

To my side.

He came right up behind me, pressing his chest against my back. His hands moved to the counter, gripping it with his large hands. His knuckles popped up, and his forearms were corded with veins. His breath fell on the back of my neck, and when he pressed into me a little harder, I could feel the outline of his dick.

His fat dick.

I hadn't paid attention the last time he was on top of me. I was in a state of panic, terrified that this strange man was going to fuck me on the bedroom floor. But now I stared down at the bowl of scrambled egg whites in front of me, feeling the definition of his thick cock in his sweatpants. He was definitely bigger than Egor, definitely bigger than any other man I'd had before.

No wonder he was so arrogant.

He stayed there, his hard chest pressing against me every time he took a breath. His hands gripped the counter harder, his knuckles starting to turn white. I could feel the heat radiate from his body, the need to take me right in the middle of his kitchen.

I waited for him to move, but it was obvious he was going to stay in that exact spot until I pulled him tighter or pushed him off. "What are you doing?"

"Exactly what you want me to do."

I looked at him over my shoulder. "I never said I wanted you."

He pressed his mouth against my ear, his breath audible in my ears. "But you haven't pushed me away either."

I swallowed the lump in my throat, my palms becoming sweaty for no reason at all.

"And we both know you have no problem throwing me off." He pressed me farther into the counter, caging me like an animal. He breathed louder into my ear canal, his lips brushing against my hairline. "I see the way you look at me. I see the way you pretend you don't want me when you really do. So let's stop pretending." He angled his neck down and gave me a kiss on the neck, right over my pulse. It was short and simple, just a brush of his lips against my hot skin, but I could feel the softness of his lips, the coarseness of his facial hair. A slight tremor moved down my spine, a natural response that I couldn't control. It all happened so quickly, and I felt a rush I hadn't felt in so long.

Arousal.

I hadn't wanted a man in years. Sex was a chore that I had to do every day. It was torture, to have a man like Egor inside me, to dump his seed within me against my consent. It was painful and abrasive, making me bleed because I was always so dry.

But now, the idea of sex wasn't unappetizing. It was exciting and adventurous like it used to be.

Carter changed everything with that simple kiss.

He pulled his mouth away and hovered there, absorbing my reaction like a sponge. He released the counter then wrapped his arms around my waist, securing his powerful muscles around me like ropes made of metal. He squeezed me against him, his cologne heavy in my nose. He breathed into my ear again, his arousal obvious in the way his hands shook slightly. "It'll be different with me." His lips brushed against the shell of my ear when he spoke. "I'll make you come—every time."

It was a bold promise to make, especially since orgasms weren't necessarily synonymous with sex. I never had them with Egor, obviously. But the men in my past didn't deliver them on a regular basis either. Carter had a different level of confidence, either because of his size or because of his experience.

For a second, it was actually tempting.

Then the logic descended, and I pushed away the fog Carter created. I didn't want this. I didn't want to give Carter a reason to tighten his hold, to not want to release me. I had to escape, to get back to where I belonged. "Get off me, Carter." I kept my voice steady, doing my best to seem as sincere as possible.

His hands squeezed me a little harder, like he had no intention of letting me go.

I held my breath, unsure what would happen.

Then he pulled his arms away and moved toward the dining room, listening to my request like he said he would. "I heard what you said." He turned around to look at me before he walked into the dining room. "But we both know you don't mean it."

TWENTY-TWO

Carter

I'd had rescued slaves stay at the house with me before, but none of them ever caught my attention. Not just because they were rescued slaves, but because there was no attraction there. Anytime I went to a bar or other event, I always went home with someone. Maybe women thought I was charming, or maybe they were just impressed by my money and cars. But whatever the reason, I didn't care.

Getting laid wasn't difficult.

So my attraction to Mia wasn't based on convenience. I could get another woman if I just wanted to get my dick wet. On top of that, this woman was a victim of rape and abuse. Why would I want to be with a woman with that baggage when I could have someone else?

No clue.

But I wanted her all the same.

Some men might have thought of her as damaged goods, but that wasn't how I viewed her. Instead, I saw a woman who didn't bow to any man, regardless of the cruelty he put her through. She kept her dignity and never stopped fighting. Victims usually lost their minds before their bodies gave out on them, but she managed to protect her cognition with flying colors.

Most people couldn't endure the kind of things she'd seen.

Couldn't stand being imprisoned by someone like Egor.

But she did it, her head still held high.

I admired her.

In addition to that, she was stunning. The scars on her back made me more attracted to her, attracted to her endurance. I wanted to be the one to hurt her, to give her my own set of bruises. But I also wanted to be the one to make her feel good, to enjoy sex before Egor claimed the prize he'd bought.

I knew she wanted me too.

I could tell by the way she looked at me, the way she brushed off my comments even though they got to her. When I pressed myself against her, she wouldn't hesitate to push me off if she didn't want me there. She wasn't afraid to fight for herself. So when she did nothing, I knew she liked it.

I knew she liked my hard dick against her ass.

She said she didn't want me, but she was lying to me as well as her to herself. I wasn't going to force her, not until she violated my rules. The second she crossed me, I wouldn't hesitate. She would be on her back and in my bed, her legs spread and her pussy full of my come. But until that moment, she was still free to call the shots.

I wasn't stupid. I knew a woman like her wouldn't settle for being a prisoner forever. Eventually, she would make her move. She would either try to kill me or try to run. Based on our chemistry, she probably wouldn't try to murder me. I'd been kind to her in comparison to Egor, so she would probably feel too guilty to pull that stunt.

That gave her only one other option—to run.

And when she did, I would be ready for her.

I was in my office with the door shut when I called Conway.

He answered after a few rings. "Are you ever going to come and visit me?"

"I told you I had my hands tied."

"You mean, your hands *full*."

Full with tits, he meant. "I'm guessing you're alone right now?"

"My father is working in the office while my mom took Sapphire to look at houses in the area."

"You're letting the women make that kind of decision? Are you really that bedridden?"

"My ribs are still in bad shape," Conway answered in a deep voice. "The doctor said these kinds of breaks take a while. I think it'll be another few weeks before I'm back to my full health. I've been purposely taking it easy because I want to be in the best shape possible when Sapphire goes into labor."

Now it all made sense. Conway wasn't the kind of guy who slowed down just because his body gave out on him. "Gotcha."

"Still have your little pet staying with you?"

"Yep. A few more weeks."

"Still a handful?"

"She's not so bad. I made a deal with her."

"What kind of deal?" he asked, full of intrigue.

"I told her if she behaved herself, I wouldn't beat her and rape her." I'd never struck a woman or took one against her will in my life, but I felt differently about Mia. Now I was looking for an excuse to have her, especially when I knew she wanted me to.

"Sounds like a pretty good deal."

"But I'm hoping she doesn't follow the rules…"

He chuckled into the phone. "I bet you are. What constitutes good behavior?'"

"Not trying to escape or kill me."

"That should be easy to follow."

"She's not that kind of woman. She jumped out of my car when I first bought her from the Underground, and she's told me off more times than I can count. She's not the kind of woman to settle for anything less than what she deserves."

"So which one do you think she'll do? Run or kill you?" he asked. "Personally, I hope it's the latter."

"Ha," I said sarcastically. "Without me around, you wouldn't know what to do with yourself."

"I've got a wife and a kid. I'm plenty entertained."

"Are you entertained right now?" I asked. "Your wife and baby took off to buy a house."

"To look at a house," he corrected. "And I don't give a shit where we live. As long as she's happy, I'm happy. So, which one do you think she'll do?"

"I don't think she'll try to kill me. She's no match for me, and she's got a soft spot for me."

"You said the same thing about me, but you're dead wrong."

I grinned at my cousin's comment. "I'm definitely right about her. She wants me. She just won't admit it."

"What makes you so sure?"

"Trust me, I know when a woman wants me." They were usually more forward and open about it than Mia was, but my instinct was right on point.

"If that's the case, why haven't you nailed her?"

After everything she'd been through, it was probably hard to imagine enjoying sex. It probably felt wrong to want me in the first place, considering that I bought her from an underground slave auction. "I'm sure it doesn't feel right to her."

"Why do you want her anyway? You can pick up pussy anywhere."

There was something special about Mia. "Yeah, I know. But there's something about Mia that I can't stop thinking about. She's one hell of a woman. I understand why Egor paid so much to get her back."

"She's that sexy?" he asked incredulously.

"And she's full of fire, fury, and passion. When I first got her, I had to scare her into submission. I ripped off her clothes and pinned her to the ground. I've seen the scars on her back. It looks like someone whipped her until all her skin was removed. I felt bad for her, obviously. But I also wanted to give her those scars myself…" I wouldn't have admitted that to anyone but Conway. It was a twisted thing to say, but Conway knew I had special kinks. I'd always been into submissive women, but he never had been.

"Carter, you do realize she's your slave, right? Walk into her room and do whatever you want."

She was my property at the moment, so I had every right to treat her that way. Egor didn't care if I used her, and I could enjoy her until I had to give her back. But since that was innately wrong, I couldn't go through with it. "I want to…but I want to be better than that. We saved hundreds of women before her. If I resort to that…I'm just as bad as the other assholes that buy women like livestock."

"We were never in it to save women. We were in it for the money. I know it—you know it."

"But I'm not evil." There was nothing I wanted more than to fulfill my secret fantasies, to take a woman, hurt her, and do whatever I wished. The women I bedded were into kinky stuff, but never something as taboo as slavery. This woman was literally a prisoner. It couldn't get more taboo than that.

"Since you're giving her to Egor in a few weeks, I don't think it makes a difference what you do with her. It's not like you bought her for yourself with the intention of keeping her until you made her dig her own grave. It really doesn't matter. If that's where she's going, none of this matters. And if she really does want you, it might be a nice vacation for her…before she has to go back."

That was another reason why I didn't want to start fucking her, especially if it was consensual. It would make it more difficult for me to hand her over in a few weeks. If she broke my rules and ignited my temper, then I would have to keep my word and fulfill the promise I made. It would be just about sex, about chaining her to my headboard and doing whatever I wanted. I wouldn't feel bad about taking her how I wanted, not when I gave her a way to avoid it. "I don't want to feel anything for her. I have to give her back to Egor. After what happened with the Skull Kings, I can't make an enemy out of this guy. He's too unpredictable. So I can't change my mind about the commitment I made. It would be easier if she defied me and I had to punish her. I wouldn't feel bad about what I was doing since I gave her an out in the beginning."

"So if she tries to escape, you'll get what you want?"

"Exactly."

Conway fell quiet, his mind obviously working in the silence.

"What are you thinking?" I asked.

"I was thinking that you want her to break the rules…so why don't you make that happen?"

"I can't make her do anything. That doesn't even make sense."

"Think about it," he said. "Let her think you've dropped your guard. Let her think you're distracted. Let her think she has a real chance. Pretend to forget to turn on the alarm at night. Pretend it's possible for her to get out."

My interest increased as the arousal coursed through my veins. If I let her believe she could really make it out of here, and even gave her another warning that she shouldn't make the attempt, I wouldn't have to feel any guilt as I enjoyed her. She could do everything right, but I would be waiting for her—in the darkness. I would grab her, watch the hope disappear from her eyes, and then I would take her to bed—where she belonged.

Then I could finally have her—guilt-free.

I could fuck her hard.

I could spank her hard.

Slap her hard.

And do whatever I damn well pleased.

"What do you think?" Conway asked, bringing my attention back to the conversation.

My hand tightened into a fist because my desire outweighed my conscience. I didn't consider myself to be a bad man, but I never claimed I was good either. I was a descendant of a line of criminals. My dad never professed to be a good man. Even to this day, he didn't claim that he was. All he ever said was that he loved his family…and that was the only good quality he possessed.

I was no different. "I think it's the best idea you've ever had."

CPSIA information can be obtained
at www.ICGtesting.com
Printed in the USA
LVHW041815140319
610673LV00002B/237

9 781725 639164